We Met In The Fog Book Two

Kam Kovah

Grace Edgewood

Edited by Grace Edgewood

Author photo: Olivia Merritt

Interior design by Grace Edgewood

Cover design by Grace Edgewood

ISBN: 979-8-9859016-2-7

—For Piper, Tenley, and Reese—

We Met in the Fog

"You can't go back and change the beginning,

but you can start where you are and change

the ending."

— C.S. Lewis —

Table of Contents

Chapter One:

Welcome to Eztenburg

I didn't have time to whisper a prayer. All I could do was close my eyes and brace for impact.

As I rounded the corner and came into sight of Town Square, a shadow shifted in the entrance of an alleyway. I tripped headlong and landed sprawled on the dirt. The rough cobblestones bruised my ribs and arms as I crashed downward. My mouth tasted blood, and dirt stung my eyes.

A voice growled at me from the darkness as I gathered myself. "Get up," said the voice that haunted my nightmares.

A hand grabbed my shirt collar and rolled me over, giving me my first look at the figure looming over me. He was tall, almost a head taller than I was. His sandy hair had fallen out of its bun when he grabbed me. His deep blue eyes raged like a stormy sea. I could have sworn flashes of lighting hid in those eyes. Despite his small stature, he greatly outsized me. With his fist gripping my shirt, he dragged me into the narrow space between two buildings.

"Rowan—" I started to protest.

He shoved me back down into the dirt. "It's *Jaggar* to you, Kovah." He spit my name back at me like venom.

"What do you want today?" I asked quietly, trying to keep my eyes downcast. The grass here was worn thin. His shoes kicked up clouds of dirt every time he shuffled.

"I want you to take back what your father said about me last night."

"But—"

He kicked me in the stomach and cut me off. "I said, take it back."

"What did he say?" I gasped. My eyes watered, and my stomach clenched. I feared my breakfast might make a reappearance.

"You are going to make me repeat it?"

"Yes—I mean, no… I—" this should have been easier. It only happened after *every* council meeting. I wasn't sure if Jaggar Senior forced his son to do the dirty work or if Rowan volunteered. I could picture his grin when his father told him of the atrocities at the meeting. Rowan got some kind of sick glee out of making me miserable. "I'm sure he didn't mean it," I mumbled, hating myself more by the minute.

He kicked some dirt in my face. "Did you say something?"

"I'm sure he didn't mean it," I said only a little louder.

"But do *you* mean it?"

I paused, hoping he'd drop the subject if I didn't answer. He kicked my shin hard enough to bruise before asking again. I shook my head sadly and muttered, "No."

"Good." He dropped my shirt collar, and I sank back to sitting on my knees. Just when I thought the violence was over, he turned and planted his foot on my shoulder. He pushed hard, and I went sprawling. I waited for more punches, curses, and pain, but none came.

"See you next week," he muttered as he stepped over me.

I wiped my running nose and rolled onto my back. I took a shuddering breath and slowly sat up. My ribs were still sore from last week's council meeting. My breath caught when I put a hand to my side. I stood up slowly, trying to blink away the stars. I bent down and picked up my notebook, which had been slung from my satchel upon my initial fall. The bag was a few feet farther in the shadows. I slung the shoulder strap over my head and took a deep breath.

I stepped out of the little alleyway and into the bright morning sunlight. I swiveled my head, looking for Rowan. While he was long gone; the gawking mouths and judging stares, however, were ever-present.

This was Eztenburg.

We were only a day's boat ride from the mainland, yet we never ventured there. When it wasn't raining, hailing, sleeting, or thundering, the sky hung oppressively low and left permanent fog shrouding Odin's Ridge, the tallest mountain on the island. The weather was wet, cloudy, dreary, and pretty much always the same. The people here were even more so. We all had the same sloped foreheads, broad shoulders, brooding voices, sandy blonde hair, with eyes like the ocean. Each generation of Eztenburg citizens looked more and more alike until even their mothers started confusing their children with their neighbors' children.

The town square was bustling today, all those similar people doing the same business with their usual customers. People walked to and from the clearing just outside on the cobbled streets while the vendors hustled people into buying overpriced cloth or fruits. People shouted while animals bleated and croaked. The rising chorus coming from the town was enough to make a man go deaf.

Luckily, I worked on the fringe of the square. It was one of the few shops to survive outside the hustle and bustle of the roaring crowd. Other shops came and went as the needs faded out. Everyone needed the workshop. Whether it was a broken clock or a shattered wheel, Birger could fix it.

Birger was my father's only friend and one of the oldest property owners in Eztenburg. He owned the little shop of all trades. Most people liked him, but everyone respected him. As rumor has it, he won the land in a back alley game of charades. His winning role was a somewhat drunken version of Odin himself. He took the deed for the land and began building immediately. Eztenburg was never the same again.

I got the job as an apprentice because he and my father were friends even before the Odin impression. Rowan had randomly showed up on the workshop's doorstep one day in an apron holding a bag of tools in one hand and a bag of jiggling coins in the other, which he promptly gave to Birger. Being a clever businessman, Birger took on the extra set of hands and stowed away the bribe money for a rainy day.

I followed the narrow road that wound between vacant businesses until I saw the old wooden door to Birger's workshop. It hung slightly crooked on his hinges, with the top never touching the door frame but the bottom always dragging the floor. I sighed and turned the handle. I had to drive my shoulder into the grain of the wood to get it to open. As I hefted, I pulled the handle upward. The grinding sound was still severe, but the door was easier to open.

As I shoved my back against the door, trying to get it to close, I gave Rowan a wry nod. He gave me a cruel smile and turned back to shining the saddle he was working over. His perfect hair was already pulled back for the day's work, and his apron hung around his neck. After draping my satchel on the peg by the door, I took down my own apron and tied it behind my back.

"Kam!" a booming voice shouted from the back storeroom. "Get in here and finish sharpening this plow! I don't pay ya to sit around staring off into the sky!"

I grimaced before lugging the plow from the place along the back wall, where I'd left it the night before, to the work table by the window. From my hidden position in the back, I could hear my boss lumbering around the cramped workshop and stomping into the lobby area.

I caught a glimpse of him as he walked out the back door for more firewood. He was a rather large man with broad shoulders and a thick apron which did nothing to hold in his bulging gut. His mustache was blonde and bristled, but his head was nearly shiny and slick. Four measly hairs poked out of the top of his head like moss on a boulder.

Turning from the doorway to the lobby, I grabbed the edge of the desk and heaved myself onto it. Now that I was sitting on the edge, I could reach the window above my desk. I unhooked the latch and pushed the shutters wide. I had a beautiful view of the baker's stone wall. The aromas leaking out their back door filled my window with smells of heaven. I shimmied closer to the edge of the desk and jumped down, stumbling as my feet hit the floor. After examining the splintered handle of the plow, I gathered the spare wood from a box under my desk and retrieved my tools from my belt.

After a quick review of the splintered handle splint, I knew what needed to be done. It was almost as if the tools spoke to me as I worked. I put the plow on my desk with the handle well sticking off the side. I selected the biggest hammer from my belt and reared back. With one hand on the blade of the plow to keep it from jumping up and landing on my toe, I swung and struck the damaged wood. It cracked and left a clean fissure. One more swing took the end of the handle off. I hefted the plow further onto my desk and took the smaller piece of wood to the big piece of sandpaper in the corner.

I kept my eyes on the wood as I drug it repeatedly across the rough surface, smoothing out any splinters. My ears and my mind seemed to run around without my consent. As I worked, I could hear Rowan working at his desk. His labored breathing cut through the air like lightning, alighting on my ears. He grunted as he lifted something, and my eyes flitted up to see him lumbering into the main room of the shop. A battle axe swung over his shoulder, and a shield on his arm. We'd had a sudden influx of old weapons brought in for upkeep. Just yesterday, I sharpened a single-sided sword and added a new leather grip to it. The whole village must be redecorating with war as its theme.

Once I'd polished both the remaining handle and the broken piece, I gathered the rest of my tools. A few reused strips of cloth, a bucket of foul-smelling sap, and a thick paintbrush long past its prime. I held the broken piece of the shaft and layered on a thick coat of the sap mixture to where it would touch the handle. I carefully placed the pieces back together and pressed hard enough to squeeze out the excess sap. Using the cloth strips, I ensured the handle would remain tightly packed as it dried.

Careful not to grab it by the healing crack, I carried the plow to the back of the workshop where Rowan had been only a few minutes earlier. There, I heaved the blade onto the whetstone, a circular rock hard enough to sharpen any blade. My arms trembled from holding the weight of the plow as I drug it repeatedly over the stone's surface. Once the blade was satisfactory, I drug it near the shop doorway and dropped into the seat in front of my desk. A slight breeze wafted through and brushed across my face. I might have sworn that stream erupted from my cheeks.

I always chose the worktable with the window. It wasn't just the extra lighting and the occasional breeze; it was the freedom from the confines of the workshop. The walls were so close and the ceiling so low. I would have to stoop like

Birger if I was not so short. Birger had given me this table, but if someone else wanted it, they took it. I submit this morning's scuffle with Rowan as evidence as to why. The empty table in the back was the equivalent of Heimdall's flames.

After my quick break for water, I went to check how the handle was holding up. I walked into the central part of the shop-the area where the customers entered, thinking only of all the work I would have to do over if the sap didn't hold. I grabbed the plow and hefted it over my shoulder, praying that, when I got it back to my desk, it would be hardened properly.

"A-hem!" said an unfamiliar voice. My stomach dropped into my boots and I jumped so hard the plow slipped off my trembling shoulder. It fell to the floor with a loud *thwap*! My toes felt like they were alive with electricity after seeing how close they'd come to being chopped off. Face burning and hands shaking, I allowed my eyes to flick up to who caused me to jump.

A girl stood impatiently by the counter. "M—Ms…?" I stuttered. I heard footsteps thundering towards us, in a matter of moments, Birger would come busting in the room, probably swinging a battle axe.

"Cummins." She supplied. "Audra Cummins."

I'd seen her around town before. She was about my age, with long, loose blond hair that was pulled back at the base of her neck. Little braids spiderwebbed throughout her hair like cracks in a window pane. Her eyes were just like everyone else's, blue. But her icy eyes were like wells of anger that might never run dry. Her clothes were worn thin and had several mismatched patches. Fuzz from the sheep she shepherded coated her pants. Her frame was thin, and her clothes hung off of her, only managing to cling to her by the belt strapped around her midsection. She looked as poor as they come, but she didn't try to hide it. She wore it like a badge of honor. She held her head high and placed her hands on her hips.

Birger came crashing through the back door with murder in his eyes. He eyed the plow, then the sizable dent in his floor, and finally at me. The murder in his eyes lessened but didn't dissipate. My eyes glanced over his scowling face, around Audra's searching eyes, and found the handle of my plow.

"Do—do you need something?" I asked stupidly, trying to ignore Birger in the corner.

"Yes," she replied curtly. "My father needs his sword returned."

"Y—yes, of course. Which one was it?"

She pointed to a long single-edged sword leaning against Birger's desk. I picked it up with minor difficulty. Birger retreated to the shadows now that he was certain no one had impaled themselves. She watched me with a side-eye as I tucked the sword into its sheath.

"W—Why do you need your sword sharpened?" I said sheepishly. "We aren't at war, are we?" I had meant it as a joke, but she didn't seem to take it as one.

She grabbed the sword from my hand and fastened it to her belt like she was marching into battle. "Some of us are," she mumbled, casting an eye to the door behind me. She slowly walked out the door, peering at me with narrowed eyes. I watched curiously as she went. She closed the door sharply, which did nothing to help the broken hinges.

"Quite the odd one, she is," said a quiet voice behind me.

My heart leaped into my throat. I gripped the counter and threw a look behind me. Rowan was standing in the shadowed doorway. How long had he been there?

"Did I scare you, Kovah? Think I'm the boogeyman?" He let out a cruel laugh and disappeared back into the storeroom.

I took a hesitant breath before walking to the front door and opening it carefully. I'm not sure what I expected. Perhaps I thought she would be waiting outside, ready to answer my questions, or maybe I expected a note explaining why nothing made sense. The only thing waiting for me was a cool breeze and the threat of rain.

I turned and tried to straighten the door on its crooked hinges. The bottom of the door still hit the frame, while the top didn't touch at all. I sighed.

"Kam!" I heard Birger yell. "Get back in here, lad, and explain this dent in my floor!"

I took one last look at the packed square, then headed inside for my doom.

Chapter Two:

The Gods' Play-thing

When I re-entered the shop, Birger was waiting for me. "Ya scared me half to death, lad! Thought you'd been hurt!"

"I—I didn't mean to."

"What happened?"

"I—she, well… "

My face burned as Rowan walked past us, whistling a carefree tune. He caught my eye. "Be a man, Kovah. Go finish sharpening that plow. At least then, when you drop it, Birger will have a reason to treat you like a baby." He gave me a grin as he walked back to the storeroom. I averted my eyes from Rowan and found Birger's watchful gaze.

Birger's face burned. Even his bald head seemed to get redder. "I'd fire that creature of Heimdall if he didn't… " He trailed off, waving his fist in the air at no one in particular. Then he met my eyes, and his face softened.

"So what if you look like a talking fishbone?" He said with a grin as he thumped me on the back. "You are just as much a man as I am."

A sarcastic smile spread across my face as I rolled my shoulders from the blow. "Thanks, Birger, very encouraging."

"He'll come around, eventually… maybe he'll just overlook you like everyone else."

"How much of me can one person handle?"

"I don't know, but I'm at my limit." His lips parted in a smile, showing off his bucktooth grin.

"Good to know," I muttered. I turned to leave, but he put a hand on my shoulder.

"The Levors just brought in a music box they need fixing. I'm working on the stage for the picnic tomorrow. It should be simple. Think you could handle it?"

"No problem, boss," I could feel his stare as I stooped to grab the plow. He shuffled behind the desk as I stooped to grab the plow. As I walked hunched under the weight of the tool, I felt tools and strips of leather brush just above my head. That was one asset to being short. My thick shoes were scuffed on the toes. The worn wooden boards creaked under my slow-moving feet. I stepped around the corner to find Markus draping a piece of ragged cloth over my name etched on the work desk.

His honey-hued hair was cut short, unlike Rowan's and my own. Markus's father was a friend of Jaggar. Although the sudden hire wasn't as outright as Rowan's, I suspected

Jaggar had paid Birger to hire him. Of course, Birger would never admit it, but his silence makes one wonder.

I put the plow down inside the door, shaking the soreness from my hands. Markus looked up from the axe he was repairing and gave me a sly smile. “Need me to lift something, noodle arms?”

“You’re hilarious,” I quipped.

He leaned on the table—*my* table and grinned. “Why’d you stop by?” he asked, pretending to look around me.

I looked at the table and pointed at where my name should be. “Oh, my father’s given it to me as an early birthday present,” he said, picking up the axe. He was repairing the damaged grip and doing a poor job at it. The leather peeled away from the wood shoulder and pommel. The first time he threw it, the grip would split down the side and fly off. The edge was razor sharp and t-shaped. The butt of the blade had a swooping rune shaped like an arrow seared into it. It meant warrior, but I doubt Markus or his father had ever seen battle. How old was this axe?

Single-edged," Markus explained, "but I sharpened the back of the beard too, for extra range. What do you think, Kovah? Want to join me in target practice?" He had a malicious glint in his eyes. My face flushed, and I shook my head. He still had the axe in his hand, but I reached out and flipped up the edge of the cloth covering my name. He pretended to be baffled as he uncovered the rest of it.

"Kovah! Have you been in here with your girlfriend? I think I can see a heart next to this, look!"

I leaned forward, and the axe swooped down, a breath from the tip of my nose. The blade stuck in the wood just above my name. I jerked back and hit my head against the doorframe as he cackled. "Sorry, little Kovah, it must have slipped."

My heart beat wildly in my chest as I shrank back, wishing I could escape. I couldn't leave without a project to work on. I didn't dare stoop to grab the plow again; I couldn't put my back to him for that long. Then I saw my chance. The music box was sitting near the edge of the desk, the faded blue paint glowing in a patch of sunlight. I grabbed the music box and clutched it to my chest, preparing to run.

"Was I not clear the first time, Kovah?" He swung in a wide arch, aiming to slice my chest clean open. I flung myself backward, out of his range. I hit the floor with a hollow *thump* that echoed through the shop. He laughed maliciously as I crawled backward as fast as I could, one hand still clutching the music box. I might have crawled all the way over the Eastern Cliffs if I hadn't jammed my head into the spare desk. After stopping to catch my breath and rub the sore spot forming on the back of my skull, I stood shakily up. I heaved myself on the tiny stool and tried to ignore the pounding of my heart. I sat the music box on the work surface and fished around in my apron. I found a sketchbook, my tools, a pencil, and a few dirty rags I had tucked away.

I opened the top of the music box, trying to absorb myself in the work, but the terror of Markus's blade still haunted me. More memories surfaced among the replaying images of his hungry eyes and haunting laugh. Memories I swore to leave behind. Shouting from outside our house. Doors slamming. I could vividly see my feet running over the worn wooden floor of my bedroom to the west-facing window.

Then came the screaming.

My eyes burned as tears welled up in my eyes. My breath caught in my throat, and my heart pounded in my ears. I forced air in through my nose and out through my mouth. The wails continued thrashing around in my mind like a squirrel in a cage. I expected my heart to stop any second, just like hers. One minute she was there and then…

I squeezed my eyes shut and tried to focus on breathing. The only sounds were the roar of my own heartbeat and the distant sound of screaming. I sucked down a breath, but it didn't stop the suffocating panic.

A hand clamped on my shoulder, and I nearly jumped clean out of my skin. I stumbled back and slammed against the wall, raising my arms to defend myself from whoever had come to kill me as they had done to her.

"Kam! Kam, it's me, it's alright. Kam!" Someone gently grabbed my wrists. "Kam? Kameron, can you hear me?" I opened my eyes and blinked hard. Birger was kneeling in front of me, eyes wide with fear. I felt my mouth open and close, but no words came out, only a strangled sob.

He cursed under his breath and sat me down. “You’re alright; there’s no one here but us, okay?”

I tried to breathe, but the air caught my throat.

“Look at me,” he prompted.

I closed my eyes, trying to ignore the memories bouncing around in my head, replaying over and over relentlessly.

“Look at me!” he cupped my chin and carefully turned my head towards him. “Watch me,” he whispered. He took a deep breath through his nose and then slowly let it slip out his mouth. I tried to mimic him, but my breath seemed to lodge in my throat, choking me. Sensing my panic, he shook his head softly and kept breathing slowly and routinely.

He didn't let go of me until I could speak again. "I—I heard her." I breathed.

"Who?" Birger asked gently.

I flinched, wishing I'd kept it to myself.

"It's alright, lad."

I took a shuddering breath and stared at his giant hands encompassing my own. "My mother."

Birger took a slow breath. "What did she say?" he prompted.

"Nothing," I said, closing my eyes against the flood of images that assaulted me. Birger patted my hand and knelt before me until I had the bravery to open my eyes again. When I met his eyes again, I wasn't the only one with tears in my eyes. I gave him a nod, and he stood up, his hand extended slightly.

My face burned in embarrassment as he helped me stand. “Thanks,” I murmured.

“You’d been doing so well for so long. I thought—well,”

I hung my head, trying to hide the last tear slipping from my eye. I’d half hoped these episodes were over too.

“What happened? What triggered you?”

I cringed at that word. Birger tried not to let me see the worry in his eyes, but he was never a good liar.

“It was nothing,” I lied. “I’m fine.”

He met my eyes with gentle concern. I’m no mind reader, but I would guess he thought I wasn’t so great at lying, either.

“Can I walk you home?” He offered.

“No, no, I’ll—” he cut me off and put a hand on my shoulder.

"I'll leave Jaggar's boy to man the shop. Let me see you safely home."

"No, I can stay." I finally looked deep into the gunmetal blue of his eyes. "I'm fine," I whispered, banishing the last of her words from my mind.

I knew he didn't believe me. Those caterpillar eyebrows were so tightly knitted together that it looked like one long fuzzy snake. He closed his eyes for half a second in a soundless prayer before nodding solemnly at me.

He surveyed the desk behind me before lumbering to peer into the other room with the apprentice's desks. His face flushed red as the sunrise when he saw Markus at my desk. He crossed his arms in front of his chest, probably to restrain himself from hitting something.

"Markus!" Birger barked. "Get in here."

I couldn't see much from my position in the shadows of the back wall, but I saw Markus stalk off into the showroom with Birger hot on his heels. Without a second thought, I snuck back to my desk. I took out the music box and began to fiddle with it. I ran my fingers over the tiny dancer for a moment before opening it. There was dust and grime between the gears. The metal comb that the cylinder hit to produce the noise was bent. That was probably the final straw that had broken it. The most likely scenario: a well-meaning child had turned the lever in the wrong direction, and the cogs couldn’t stand the tension.

I took a deep breath as I reached for my smallest screwdriver, trying not to think about what had just happened. After unscrewing the comb, I took out my pliers. I straightened the teeth and set them aside. I cleaned the cogs and spring housing, then reattached the many parts and tightened the comb back into place. Finally, I released the breath I didn't know I was holding.

I closed the bottom up and turned the lever. There was a moment of nothing but whirring gears, then the notes of "Balter's Ballad" began to pour out. It was a popular drinking song that was hauntingly sad. But as the music poured out of the tiny wooden box, it wasn't drunken men I heard singing. The soft notes flowing out were sung by a familiar and sober voice: my mother's. I slammed the lid shut, cutting off the tune. Tears welled in my eyes yet again. Even without the music to accompany her song, she sang out the words in my memory.

Master of the Sea, I beg your help.

The shore I fear, only you I trust.

Lost, I have become,

In this storm of swords.

Silence your raging breath.

Captain of the wind, guide my sail.

You are the only compass for me.

Whether sea be calm and clear tonight,

Or rough as the men's raging hearts.

My ship goes down to you tonight,

Oh god of wind and sea.

When the tune was done, The notes seemed to hover in the air before drifting away. I could see lightning flashes playing out among the slashing rain outside my window as my mother sang to me. She said each line with a half smile as if the sailor from the song wasn't begging for deliverance from a god who would never answer.

I had become so lost in the song I hadn't heard someone walk up behind me. "Look at little Kovah. Still playing with dolls and jewelry boxes, I see."

I whirled around to see none other than the great Rowan Jaggar. The son of the most important man in town. The moment his father agreed or became too senile to do his job, Rowan would replace him on the town council. It was only a matter of time before he made me bow or give him a pension from my nonexistent wages.

He sneered at me and stared at my sweat-covered brow and screwdriver the size of a grain of rice. “Why’d you even take this job?”

I clamped my mouth shut and gently closed the music box's lid.

“Why don’t we go back out in the alley? That should loosen your tongue a little.”

He pushed me back, and I slid off the stool. “I said answer me!”

"Rowan!" a voice called from outside the back door. "Did you stack these logs?"

"Perhaps I did; what's it to you?"

Birger lumbered in. "If I've told you once, I've told you a thousand times. Bark up! Keeps the rain off. Go fix it!"

"Markus did those!"

"Did I ask Mark?"

"No," Rowan growled. He stalked off to fix the lumber.

"You've got to stop helping me," I said as I brushed myself off. I picked myself up and slumped back on my stool.

"If I didn't, there wouldn't be any of you to help!"

I sighed.

"You just need to stop all… this."

"All of what?"

"This," he gestured to all of me.

"That's really helpful; thank you very much, sir. Anything else you need to tell me?"

"Quitin' time," he wiggled his eyebrows as I packed up my things "I'm being serious. If you want him to stop picking on you, then stop doing all that! Stand up for yourself; stop taking it. Be the man you were born to be." He still stood in the doorway, blocking my exit.

Finally, I stopped clearing my desk to look up at him. "How am I supposed to do that, huh? Just walk in tomorrow carrying a sword, wearing a battle helmet and plaided chest armor? My father would be so proud." I turned back to my desk and fiddled with the music box. I wished he would go away and leave me alone, but I was too afraid to voice it.

"Stop letting him walk all over you," he said softly. "One day, there won't be any more for him to walk on."

"That doesn't make any sense."

"I'm trying to teach you a lesson! Just stop. Stop *this*. Moping and being meek. There was a time when you would have gladly swung back at a bully. Now…"

"I know, Birger."

"Can I do anything for you?"

"No," I slid off my stool and edged around him. I kept my eyes downcast. "I'll do better."

I could feel his eyes on me as I walked out. I still pulled up on the handle, hoping to fix the door. It did nothing to fix it. I pulled the door shut behind me and took a deep breath.

He was right of course, but I didn't see how that helped me much. I was just a toy that the gods loved to play with. I imagined they loved watching what misfortunes they could get me into.

Chapter Three:

Home Again

I scuffed my boots on the cobblestone circle outside the shop, not wanting to go home but unable to stay here. Rowan snapped the door open behind me and sneered as he disappeared into the crowds. Markus would be next. I couldn't face him again, so I gathered my courage and started the journey home. While walking through the clearing beside the square, I kept my head down, trying to walk unseen. This is where the temples were kept. People from all walks of life gave offerings of all kinds to the eight temples in the circle.

On one side of the circle, there was the Aesir. The four temples included the housing for Odin, of course, the king of all gods. The roof was sloped and had delicate carvings in the eves. Our hunters often took the eyes of their prey inside as an offering to appease his anger at losing his own.

Beside it was the temple for Thor, an open-aired pavilion of sorts. It held a large fire pit with flames that danced year-round. Each member of the town gave a portion of their bounty to Thor. A few of our counsel members still came here before big meetings. Several were gathered there now.

I kept my eyes downcast as I passed the temple for Frigg. Women always gathered outside, and not all of them were decently dressed. They begged for a husband, or for a baby, or for both. It had a gently sloping roof, and the walls were made of light-colored wood.

Tyr was the only god we gave sacrifices to in order to keep him away. We asked for war to remain away, therefore, for him to stay away. His house was littered with abandoned weapons and tear-stained letters from forgotten widows.

Completing the circle were the four temples for the Vanir, but that side had become wild and overgrown. The grass seemed to part in a line down the center of the circle, leaving Odin's side pristine and overflowing with visitors. While the Njord, the king of the Vanir, ruled a wild dominion.

Nerthus's temple had always looked overgrown, being the goddess of the wild, but especially so when her admirers disappeared. Farmers stopped praying to Nerthus when bad winters spoiled crops. Older women never brought spring flowers to the temple steps because spring never seemed to come. The cracked marble pillars seemed to only be supporting the roof because of the vines holding them up.

Beside her was the temple of Odr, god of wisdom and madness. His vast library and rows of desks were unmatched. But now his stone desks, once teeming with scholars and poets, sat bare and grew moss.

Across from Frigg's temple was Freyja, goddess of death. Her dark temple of obsidian was hung with the death wreaths of burial shrines. When the wind blew through her halls, the old flowers seemed to give up the last ghost of life. The smell of dark roses and soft lilies sang over the town once more, reminding us of times gone by.

Lastly, there was Njord. His temple was challenged only by Odin's himself. It was made of stone and driftwood, but the old linens that guarded the altar still hung in tattered strips. Njord was the guardian of the lost sailors and ocean storms.

In the middle of the courtyard, straddling the line between Aesir and Vanir, there was a large metal brazier. Flames gushed out of the top, and lines of people formed around it. Since it was so close to dinner, a member of every family was there, offering part of their meal to the gods. When it was their turn, each person stepped forward, murmured a few words, and slid the food off their plate and into the fire. This was done before every significant meal, so people were brisk about getting it done. The people gathered now all stood on the worn side of the grass, the Aesir gods. It was like a brick wall stood between them and the Vanir temples.

I ducked behind a shop and out of view of the clearing for an instant. I could see the lane to my house when someone ambushed me.

Rowan slunk out from behind a temple and charged me. He stood in front of me indignantly as if he expected me to spontaneously combust. “Kovah, What are you doing?”

I shrunk back like a dog who had been kicked one too many times. “Going home.”

“Without saying goodbye?”

He swung his leg out and caught the back of my knee. I hit the ground hard. I looked up at him, preparing myself for another fight. He looked at me, then to Odin's temple. He gave a gruff sigh before growling, "We'll rematch tomorrow, Kovah."

He stalked away, keeping an eye on me. I scurried away and ran up the road. I didn't stop until I turned up the little dirt road that was hemmed in by trees on either side. Here, no one would bother me. I walked among the fir trees and the towering spruce. Pine cones scattered under my feet. Small valleys ran on either side of the dirt road where water had eroded the path. Each year the road became smaller, and the trees at the mouth of the path became wider. How long until the road was virtually undetectable? How long until people forgot about the Kovahs that used to live at the edge of town?

I daydreamed about a small boy discovering our cottage after stumbling through the forest for a bit. Hundreds of years from now, when my family name is long forgotten, maybe then someone will find peace in the deserted place.

I never did.

The trees suddenly cleared out, and our humble abode came into view. It was a modest building with a simple wooden exterior and a long sloping roof. The steep angle almost made the house look like an upside-down boat. That was preposterous, of course, and I had only seen drawings of such things.

I stumbled up the stone steps and onto the porch. It smelled damp and cold like it might rain soon. The large door swung inward and I stepped inside the dark room where my father sat. He waited for me by the fire. His back was to me, but I know he heard me come in.

"Hello, son," said my father.

I closed the door behind me. "Hey, dad," I offered weakly.

My hands drifted unconsciously to fiddle with where my tool belt should be. After finding the area empty, my hands found the outside of my thigh and bounced there.

"So… did the meeting go well?"

"No." He prodded the fire and coaxed the flames higher. His back was to me, and I couldn't tell his mood from just his tone.

I chewed my lip nervously. "Great… I'll be upstairs then—" I hurried to the stairs, but he shifted to look over his shoulder.

"Did Jaggar's boy give you any trouble today?"

His words rooted me to the spot, making me wish I'd escaped faster. "No…" he raised his large, bushy eyebrows at me, "... more than usual," I finished.

"And what did *you* do?"

I lowered my head. He stood up and walked toward me. "Tell me what he said."

"Just that not everyone agrees with your decisions in the council."

"By everyone, you mean he and his father."

"I don't know what he meant, just what he said."

He sighed and sat back down near the fire, lost in thought. I watched the light of the dancing fire play across his face. My father was a large man, built for a war he'd never seen. He had broad shoulders that barely fit through our doorways and a long beard that covered most of his chest. His hair, like most men in the village, was worn loose and long.

His hands were sculptured by the gods to wield a broadsword, but Eztenburg hadn't seen war since we'd closed our borders.

I turned away from him and scurried up the uneven stairs. At the top of thirteen stairs, there was a little landing with a singular door: my sanctuary. I pulled myself through the narrow door and quickly shut the door behind me like I was trying to lock out my shadow. I bolted the door behind me, but that wouldn't stop him from coming in if he had a mind to. It would at least force him to knock, that is if banging and shouting fell under the knocking category.

I slumped down into the chair by my desk and sighed. It had been a long day. My eyes felt heavy, not only from the long day's work but from the lack of sleep. I had been up late the night before sharpening rocks for an invention. I should be exhausted, but my mind was filled to the brim with nervous energy. It sloshed about in my brain like sewage. Every nook and cranny was filled with it, and every compartment was submerged and unusable.

I paced for a moment. I needed to find some way to relieve all of this energy. I looked out my window, saw the moon, and walked across the moonlit boards to the window. I swung wide the panes, and a cool breeze brushed past me.

I caught a glance at the woods. The moonlight shone through the trees, casting various shadow pictures on the leaf-strewn ground. The mist curled and twisted like a living thing. Sometimes the fog fell in front of my window like a curtain, completely blocking out the rest of the world. Tonight, it hung around the house like sheets of rain, barely obscuring anything but making everything look off-kilter.

Much like my mind, the fog swirled and thickened when something disturbed it. The outer fringe moped about, but I could see animals and trees hidden among the churning cycle. My imagination always seemed to get the best of me. I could almost picture men roaming around just inside the tree line. I left the window open and walked back to the desk, trying to stop the flood of images.

I ran a hand across the familiar, care-worn leather of my notebook. I leafed through a few of the pages. Nearly every inch was scribbled over. Sketches of machine parts were doodled in the margins. Experimental instructions were listed, scribbled out, then written over again. It was all my crazy ideas, functioning and otherwise, in one place. With all that dumb luck and accidental discoveries in one palace, it's hard to believe it didn't spontaneously combust. Several others just like it littered my shelves.

I flicked through the pages again. The breeze gently lifted the hair from my forehead. I closed my eyes and let my mind wander straight out the back door of this house and to the

Eastern facing cliffs. I could imagine a dark ocean, churning and rumbling with distant storms. The breeze coming off the sea ran its fingers through my hair. I stood alone on the shadowy shore while a pale splotch of moonlight fought through the clouds. I kicked off my shoes and sat on the edge of the rocks, letting my feet dangle precariously over the void. The cool air of the gentle breeze seemed to lull my soul into a trace.

I closed my eyes and put my hands firmly on the rocky edge of the cliff. After inching my body over the side, I let go. I opened my eyes and saw the salty spray reaching up to meet me. The crashing of the waves never sounded so inviting. I looked up one last time, not at the island I was leaving behind, but at the moon. The clouds parted for an instant, and I saw the man inside wink at me. I saw the water inches from my feet and took a deep breath, bracing for impact.

I jerked awake.

I pulled my face away from the desk and sat upright, a bit of drool dribbling down my chin. After swiping at it with the back of my hand, I blinked hard and rubbed my eyes. It was still dark outside. I groaned as my stiff neck protested the movement. When had I drifted off? I stretched, and my back popped in concerning places. Standing quietly, I moved to my beloved bed.

It sat on a large rope bed frame with a rectangular sack of feathery down and hay stuffed inside. The bedposts were made from the limbs of trees that had fallen years and years ago. The quilt was thick for the cold winters ahead. I traced the designs of the gods on the top with my finger absentmindedly. There was the hammer, Thor's chosen weapon. The intertwining ropes of Odin. A long boat with shields boarding the sides and sails emblazoned with a symbol I didn't recognize.

I sank into the familiar smell and weight of the quilt and closed my eyes. Would I be able to go back to sleep? My neck had a crick, and my body was sore. My mind whirled in confusing circles. I doubted I would find sleep again before the sun rose to drag me into another day.

Chapter Four:

Nervous Energy

The sun streamed into the room, blinding me momentarily. I had gone back to sleep after all. Instead of rolling away from the light, I rolled towards it and squinted out the window. The sun had already risen above the horizon. I slept much later than I intended.

I jumped out of bed and scrambled to get clothes on. With one hand, I splashed some water on my face, with the other, I ran my fingers through my hair in an effort to tame the beast. I ran out my door but skidded to a stop on the landing and tentatively called for my father. He didn't answer. The window above the sink in the kitchen was open. The soft morning music of birds wafted in.

The house was empty.

I tried not to dwell on that fact too long as I jumped down the rest of the stairs. I grabbed a piece of ham from the table. My father never cleaned up after himself in the morning. Much like me, his mind was still vacant in the morning. I had enough sense to put an extra biscuit in a sack as I raced for the door. Since my shoes had little traction on the worn boards, I slid into the door with a thud. I scrambled back to grab my satchel before tugging the giant door open.

After running down the washed-out gully and diving through the trees, I made a mad dash for the clearing. I threw my biscuit into the fire in the brazier and whispered a prayer. Instead of watching it burn, I sprinted back into the town square.

I was running full speed, the only thing on my mind was that I was late. Birger would think I was lazy, or that I didn’t care about this job. Just when I thought things couldn't get any worse, Rowan appeared from the alley in front of me. All I saw was his leg sticking out in front of me before I was on him. I plowed into him, unable to stop myself in time. We both flipped over each other and skidded to a stop on the rough-hewn cobblestone.

My heart pounded as I lay there, trying to get my bearings. I was so dead.

"Kovah," Rowan growled as he extracted himself from me. He stood up, shaking the dust from his hair and brushing off his clothes. "What were you thinking?"

"I—I'm late," I murmured, trying to stand up without putting my back to him for too long.

He wet his lips and pushed his hair out of his eyes. Our fall had dislodged his hair from its ponytail at the base of his neck. His hair now hung in loose strands around his face, framing his murderous eyes. He squared his feet and prepared to swing.

I wasn't going to survive this one. It took all my courage, but I steadied my footing, readjusted my bag, and ran for my life. I fled down the rest of the street until I saw Birger's shop. I tried to open the door and keep running but my momentum carried me straight into the door. It didn't budge. I grabbed the handle and heaved against it, pulling up on the handle as I pushed. The door scraped the floor and opened just enough for me to squeeze inside. I heaved the door closed behind me and turned to run to my desk. Instead, I ran headlong into Birger.

I jumped sharply back and collided with the doorframe. To cover my awkwardness, I used my momentum to spin and grab my apron from the hook by the door. I fumbled with my straps until I turned back and found him staring at me. Breathing heavily, I tied the last lopsided knot in my apron with a jerk and gracelessly leaned against the door.

“Where’s the fire?” he said as I tried to catch my breath.

“No fire. Everything's fine. Nothing to worry about,” I said unconvincingly. About that time, the door jumped behind me like someone was pushing on it. Probably Rowan, whom I’d stranded out in the street. I drug my heels into the ground as Rowan rammed his shoulder into the door, desperate to get in. I put my back to it and strained to keep the door from budging but it creaked open bit by bit. Finally it swung wide, pushing me into the wall. I stayed flat behind the door, praying Rowan wouldn’t see me.

“Where is he?” Rowan growled.

“Door’s pesky, ain’t it?” I felt Birger move beside me to cover the space behind the door just a little more.

"I know he's here! Tell me where he is, old man."

"Now who would that be?"

Rowan huffed in frustration and walked away. The door *whooshed* close and I was revealed for the world to see, but Rowan was gone. My knees shook and I slid to the floor.

"Careful there, lad," Birger said as I wrapped my arms around myself. I took a shuddering breath and buried my hands in my knees.

"Relax, Lad!" Birger said earnestly as he stooped to squat next to me. "He's gone, take a breath."

I shook my head. "You don't understand," I said, finally looking up, "now he's going to be like this forever." I looked up at Birger to find his eyes shining.

"You hit 'em back, didn't you?" I tried to protest but he stood up and punched his hand, hard. "Ooh, I should'a seen it coming. Where'd you do it? Was he bleedin'?"

"Birger I—"

"Coulda give me warning, lad, I'd like to seen it."

"I didn't hit him!" I blurted out.

Birger's prancing stopped and he came to stand beside me. "Say that again?"

"I didn't hit him… I couldn't. I ran away."

He put a gentle hand on my shoulder, "It's a step in the right direction." He gave me a small smile and asked, "Did you tell your father about everything last night?"

I turned away so he wouldn't see my face flush. "I didn't see my father last night," I lied. "He got home late from a council meeting and was gone when I got up this morning."

He shook his head as I stood up and bustled past him. "Shame. He would have liked to hear about it."

I shot him a look. "No, he would have asked me why both of us were virtually unharmed after Rowan and I fought."

I put my hands on my hips and deepened my voice to my father's octave. "You should be married by now! Stop fiddlin' with your inventions and get on with your life. You should ask someone from the council for their daughter's hand. Stop being picked on and start a fight! Inflict some damage!"

Birger laughed. "It's not that he can't stand *you*. It's your choices that he hates."

"Wow, thanks for putting that in perspective there, boss," I said as I glumly gripped the counter. I turned around to lean against it as my eyes roamed the room. A shadow passed in front of the window. A newly tied ponytail bounded behind a figure with squared shoulders and clenched fists. My heart beat wildly as I tried to think of a plan. Birger saw my fear and grabbed me by the front of my shirt. He threw me in a tiny closet by his desk. I tripped over a bucket and broom and crashed into the wall. I had enough time to see him wince for me before he slammed the door.

The only light slipped in through the crack at the bottom of the door. I shuffled backward, trying to hide from that sliver, but I didn't have enough room to take a step back, let alone hide. I heard the door grind open and shut again. Birger's voice sounded from right outside the door. "You're late."

"Oh, can it, old man," Rowan growled.

There was a moment of quiet before the door creaked open. I was certain it was Rowan coming to murder me, but the large silhouette before me was Birger. He glanced behind him before pulling me out of the closet by the apron and dragging me out of the front door.

He pushed me into the little dark alley beside his shop. “If you don’t pummel that kid soon, I will,” he said, grinding his teeth.

I gave him a small smile and he dropped my apron.

“Look, lad,” he paused, rubbing the back of his neck. “There's the picnic at noon today, and you’ve already missed your check in time at the shop.” I started to protest but he put a hand to his lips. “I think you should just not come in today.”

“Birger, I’ve never missed a day in my life. I—”

Birger shook his head. He threw a thumb back at the door to the shop. “Don’t come in today.” He raised his bushy eyebrows at me, asking if I understood.

I glanced at the door to the shop. Rowan waited just inside that door. If I went home, I would be a coward. If I stayed here, he’d certainly notice me. Sooner or later he’d pay me back.

"But, I couldn't leave you here with the new influx of weapons to fix. We're practically drowning in work."

He sighed and put two big hands on my shoulder, forcing me to look up at him. "Let me rephrase: you can't come in today. Go home. Stay out of trouble until whatever big announcement at noon. I won't tell that git or your father."

My heart pounded as my hands found my apron to fiddle with. "Birger?" I finally looked up, and he met my eyes. I expected him to look down at me with anger; he was losing a valuable team member. I anticipated condescension in his gaze, after all, I was running away from another fight. When his blue eyes met mine, all I saw was tenderness and a flicker of worry.

"Now get lost, I've got a shop to manage, and you've got a whole town to avoid." After gently pushing me further into the shadows of the alley, he turned and marched through the shop door, giving me a wink as he went.

My heart pounded as I scurried up the alley and behind the old shops and houses of Eztenburg. What on earth would I do with myself? I passed the clearing where the temples stood, abandoned after the morning rush. The extra food in my knapsack suddenly felt heavier. After casting a quick glance around, I scurried to the large metal brazier and dropped a slice of ham from my breakfast and a piece of my bread. I muttered a prayer of gratitude before stumbling up the lane.

I needed to change out of my apron and the thick leather pants I always wore to protect my stick thin legs from swords, axes, fire, and every other dangerous thing in the workshop. After stumbling up the stairs to my bedroom, I slipped on simple cloth pants and a comfortable green shirt.

Today the council members had an important meeting, so my dad wasn't home. Strangely, the nature of these meetings was kept private. The final decision was to be announced at the picnic today.

There had been whispers, of course, snippets of conversations heard bouncing between the colorful stalls in the square. Murmurs stated a creature roamed the shores, warding people away from the water. Gossipers wondered if Jaggar would finally step down and let Rowan join the council. Whispers said that we would open our borders. Somehow, of all the preposterous things I'd heard, this one took the cake.

We had only closed ourselves off because of the state of the world. I didn't see how the entire world could still be in this much peril. Many eons ago, the gods sent a message to my great, great, great, great grandfather. We still had only one chief and no supporting council members back then. It was strictly bloodline, so every new chief was the son of the previous. That is until my father's father came along. He was the last chief of our clan. He established the council and its voting system. My father may not have been chief, but he was more respected than any man in town.

Anyway, this chief ancient saw a world in catastrophe. Burning buildings, screaming children, and giant waves overtaking the land. He told the whole village we should close our borders, guard our gates, and quarantine ourselves until this blew over. They all actually believed him. How gullible were my ancestors anyway?

Eztenburg had stopped all trade with outside countries and had become entirely self-sufficient. Our island was alone with our troubles and with our successes.

We never heard the news of plagues and wars that we had avoided. We never heard any news; we were isolated and separated from the world. Who knew what went on that we had missed? Now, centuries later, people really thought we could just jump right into the old circles we used to operate in.

All of our trade alliances had probably forgotten we existed. We had no significant illnesses sweeping the island. Some might argue: why should we risk all of that for the sake of exploration?

Part of me knew it wasn't wise, but the other half of me whispered to give it a try. I would be lying if I said I wasn't intrigued.

I knew what the logical decision was, and yet, my heart didn't seem to agree. The ocean always seemed a mysterious and dangerous thing, but I was drawn to it. On an island, there are not many places you can go without finding the water again. Eztenburg only inhabited half of the island, if that. The rest was a fantastic and unruly wilderness. People spoke of old times when the gods walked among us and when we lived freely across the entire island.

The green forest all around, the trees towering over me like a canopy over a bed. The moss-covered stones at my feet sang of different times, better times. I could feel the cool of the forest air on my skin and smell the dirt under my feet. A bird roosted nearby, and a deer moved through the heather.

I blinked.

I was stuffing things into a satchel to take with me but had gotten lost in thought. I returned to putting food and a water skin into my bag. I also took out my sketchbook and pencil and held them in my hands for an instant. Should I? After a moment's hesitation, I placed them gingerly inside the bag.

I couldn't fit the picnic blanket in my bag, so I tucked it under my arm. But only three steps out the door, I was tired of carrying it. I left it folded under a bush in the front yard so I could come back before the picnic and grab it without my father seeing.

No matter the decision reached today, my father would come home in a foul mood. Something was always wrong. Usually, it was Jaggar, but who knew? Maybe today, it would be someone else's ideas that made him angry. Either way, I didn't want to meet him until after the announcement.

Chapter Five:

Tumbling and Bumbling

As a child, I often snuck away to the woods to escape the loud crowds and cramped houses. The forest was teeming with life but not bustling with people. There was no one to bump shoulders with. No buildings to live in the shade of. It was open. It was free. Life in the forest consisted of deer and moss. The deer didn't judge me for wanting to be alone. The birds admired my doodles. The streams laughed with me, not at me.

Water ran rampant in the forest, and because of it, the forest grew in leaps and bounds. Here, freedom grew in abundance. After walking for nearly half an hour, I found a perfect glen. The sun was hidden behind Odin's Ridge, and the meadow was covered in plush moss. I pulled my sketchbook from my pocket and sat down on the soft moss bed that only I could enjoy. No one else in the village had this privilege. I drew the passing deer and enjoyed the open sky, even if it was overcast. I even picked a few wildflowers to press into delicate skeletons of papery beauty.

Filled with newfound confidence, I headed deeper into the woods. Maybe if I had been paying attention, I would have seen the absence of grass beyond the tall weeds just ahead of me. I might have seen the top of a tree far below me.

But I didn't.

I stumbled through a bush and found empty air waiting for me. Down I fell, like a rock into a pond. I tumbled down the slope and landed flat on my back with the breath knocked from me. Stars danced in front of my eyes as I drew deep breaths, trying to replace the air knocked from me. Coughing, I sat up to assess how badly I was hurt. I had minimal injuries, only a few stains on my clothes and some scratches on the flat of my hands. Turning my gaze to my surroundings, I found that I had come into a beautiful dell the hard way. Behind me, the steep embankment, before me, a gently sloping hill that probably led towards Odin's Ridge. A tall oak stood on the far side of the glade. A little stream trickled over some pebbles in front of me.

Even without the strange stones in the middle, I could feel the somber mood the glade held. I approached the ruins with care, trying not to fall again. It seemed to be a temple of sorts. The foundations were clearly placed with its back facing the mountain and the steps leading up the way I'd come. I walked up the crumbling stairs to behold a large marble slab coated in leaves and vines. Several fallen walls scattered the floor with rubble, but a large cornerstone still stood tall. Its roof had fallen in long ago, but this wall miraculously stayed.

As I approached, I noticed the moss covering it wasn't as full in some places. I used my hand to wipe away a portion and gasped.

Ancient runes were chiseled into stone with pictures depicting scenes of war and devastation. A man stood over a crowd of people who had their heads bowed. A woman wept in the corner. The next picture was of ruins just like these. I wiped away the grime to read the above inscription.

It read:

WHEN THEY TURNED THEIR BACKS ON US, SO DID WE.

The last discernible picture was of three pillars. The back two were a little shorter than the front one. Underneath, in large font, was the motto:

BURY THE FORSAKEN.

Something rustled in the underbrush above me. I whirled around but could see nothing but grass and a rustling bush. Turning to run, I slipped on the vines and moss, and ended up tumbling headlong to the stone floor. My shoulder exploded with pain as it landed against the temple floor. I cried out, and the rustling stopped for a moment. For just an instant, I had hope that it was only a deer. Then I rolled over and saw a boot emerging from the thistle. Putting one hand on my shoulder, I bolted, unwilling to meet this stranger eye to eye.

Chapter Six:

Picnic Drama

I ran.

I ran past a glade of flowers, a pond, and a willow tree. After I was confident no shadowy figure was following me, I paused to catch my breath. Chest heaving, I sat heavily on a log and looked up into the tree canopy. A jolt went through me when I realized it was nearly noon. Again I started running, but this time towards the house. After grabbing my blanket from under the bush, I turned on my heel and headed for town. Once I joined the throngs of people maneuvering for the meadow, I slowed to a walk.

I hadn't missed it after all. After finding a relatively empty area, I spread out my blanket. I plopped down and caught my breath while everyone else settled around me. There was a young boy nearby who was chasing a butterfly. A recently married couple sat with intertwined hands and closely pressed bodies. I noticed Jaggar strutting from the Town Hall like he owned the whole island. A quick scan of the area confirmed that Rowan was nowhere to be seen.

Everyone was getting nervous, and I was beginning to get fidgety. I retrieved my water and took a sip, just to have something to do. I watched the boy chasing the butterfly again. He wandered close to me, and I smiled at him. He didn't seem to see me. His butterfly had just discovered it could fly up and away from him. I grabbed the bug and gently put it into his hand.

The stunned butterfly sat there momentarily as if to get its bearings. The boy smiled up at me with dimpled cheeks and wide ocean eyes. The butterfly got away from him, and he took off running again.

I watched him with mild amusement. His tiny legs couldn't go much faster than a toddle, so the butterfly kept getting ahead of him.

I choked mid-swig when my father walked past me. I coughed and gagged on my water, but he didn't so much as look at me. I swallowed my water again and sat back on my hands. My stomach churned. He must be angry with me, furious, and so disappointed. Had Birger told him about Rowan? About yesterday? The smile died on my face. He strode to the middle of the clearing and looked around at us.

"Friends, neighbors, and fellow councilman: let us eat!"

There were cheers and whoops as people brought out sack lunches and sleeves of wine. I fished my squashed sandwich out of my bag and tore a chunk off the corner.

I joined the line that was forming in front of the large bonfire. We each took a turn selecting a piece of our meal to throw in. Some people mumbled thanks to a specific god, while others simply dropped their offering and walked away. I chose the latter option. I lowered my offering and strolled back to my blanket. Everyone seemed on edge. We were all worried about what this new decree might mean. People sat in small huddles and scarcely talked to anyone outside of their group.

When I reached my blanket, I found that everyone seemed repulsed by me. All the surrounding blankets had been pulled backwards. Did I smell that bad? Surely not, I hadn't even worked in the shop today. Ignoring my bruised feelings, I sat alone and nibbled on the sandwich. My gaze swept across the field of heads. I was keen to observe but quick to avoid anyone's stares. My eyes settled on the table where the councilman sat. My father was red in the face, and his fists were clenched. Jaggar stood behind him. I could faintly see his mouth moving.

My father barked something back at him. Jaggar became angry. His eyebrows knit together, and he shifted farther behind my father. My father's eyes widened, and he growled back a response. Jaggar's eyes frantically swept the congregation. His eyes met mine, and he smiled. He whispered something in my father's ear, who in turn searched the field until he found me. His face hardened and he nodded reluctantly.

I looked away, unsure of what exchange had just taken place. Maybe I shouldn't have come at all. A silence settled over the field and I looked up to find my father taking center stage in front of the council's table. He awkwardly stood, wetting his lips and shaking out his hands. He stood on the edge of the stage and looked out at me. For once, I wasn't the one who looked away.

"Silence!" he boomed, despite the fact the birds had already fallen silent. It felt like even the gods above were leaning down to hear what he had to say. "The council has made a decision." I sat forward. My father looked back to the table of elders. I saw Jaggar give a slight nod. When my father turned back toward the crowd, I saw Jaggar smile.

"No," I whispered. I rocked forward onto my knees as if I could outrun the decision. Something in my stomach churned uncomfortably. Even though I didn't know what the decision was, the air had the foretaste of danger.

"As a council, we have decided… " he risked a look back at the other members who shifted uncomfortably in their chairs. "We have decided to abolish the old way and forge a new road."

An explosion of murmurs echoed across the field. What on earth could that mean? Why such a drastic change? Every tongue had the same word rolling off it. *Why?*

I leaned back, resting my rear on my feet, still in a ready position to run.

"Eztenburg," he continued. My eyes shot up to focus on him. "When is the last time any of the old gods answered your prayers?" My father didn't sound like himself. His tone was flat, and his face was slack. Only his eyes were cast upward. He seemed to be praying while he spoke. "Why should we honor them, when they ignore our offerings and our pleas?" Murmurs and shouts broke out among everyone gathered. My father tried to speak over them. "A brigade will be constructed to demolish any relics to these old gods." He took a breath and half heartedly added, "You can volunteer for a place in the army tomorrow at the Town Hall."

"Come on, Kovah!" A man yelled.

Hearing his name seemed to awaken him again. He rubbed his hands together nervously and answered the man. "I hear you, Rudric, but as a *counsel*, we needed to think about…" he looked back at Jaggar, "the future. Bury the forsaken. Move on."

I hadn't realized I was standing until now. My balled fists were shaking. *This was all Jaggar's doing. The rest of the council would never agree to this*, one part of me said. *Maybe this is a blessing in disguise*, said the other. But deep down, I knew this would never end well. I watched my father leave the angry crowds of people and walk home. For once, he and I agreed on something.

This never should have happened.

Chapter Seven: Arguing Again

I bent down hesitantly, half waiting for the people to turn on me and begin shouting. When no one paid any mind to me, I began stuffing things in my bag and hastily folding the blanket. I kept my head down and pretended not to hear the people shouting. As I turned to go, people began to notice my departure. They rushed after me, demanding answers. I refused to look anyone in the eye. My heart pounded out of my chest as they pressed in on me. Every eye seemed to scald me like fire.

I ducked under a swinging fist and scurried into the tree line. No one dared follow me into Burgess Woods. Very few knew the paths and even less had the courage to leave the town's safety. I hurried to the hidden path that led to my house. The ravines on either side of the old dirt road had deepened from last night's rain. I tried to take the path of least resistance, but the trail was still just as washed out and steep as ever. This time, I didn't mind the trek because it gave me time to get lost in my thoughts.

Abolish the old ways? Build a 'new road'? Granted, none of the gods ever answered my prayers to strike Rowan dead with lighting, but did that give me the power to pretend like they didn't exist? Why had we jumped to such extreme measures so soon? Who would join the brigade?

My thoughts were interrupted when the house came into view. Smoke billowed up out of the chimney, which meant my father was already home. Yippee. Maybe I should pray that he disappeared long enough for me to slip upstairs unnoticed. Instead of going quietly as I had prayed, I tripped on the edge of a board as I mounted the stairs to our porch and spilled the contents of my satchel. "No, no, no," I muttered, hoping no one saw, because my father had definitely heard. A compass, notebook, and several pencils went rolling across the uneven boards. I shoved it all back in and hurried to the door.

He would be in a terrible mood. I could feel the anger emanating from the house. I took a deep breath and opened the door.

"H—hey, dad," I cleared my throat to hide the tremor in it. He grunted in reply. I saw his bulking figure outlined by the glow of the dying fire. "Do you want to talk about it?" I squeaked.

"Idiots!" He roared. "Fools! All of them! Jaggar uses big words and made-up rumors and they all bend over backwards for him"

I snuck over to a chair and tried to hide my fear.

"If I were chief, I wouldn't force our youth to do this."

"What?"

"They voted for people to join his little brigade. He's calling it Hel's Horde. It's a brutish task force." He finally looked me in the eye. "Jaggars and two others voted for you."

"Can they do that?"

"Yes, but—I couldn't let that happen."

He stood up and I caught a glimpse of his face in the firelight. His jaw was bruised, and he favored a leg. He didn't look this bad at the picnic. He moved to look out the window.

"Dad… I—"

"I may have only delayed the inevitable, he will come. He tends to get his way in town." He drew the curtains shut and locked the door.

"Why is he doing this?"

"Power," he suggested. "History will prove, every time a villainous man comes to power, he finds his dominion all too small."

I was quiet for a moment. I couldn't find the words to explain the emotions rising in my throat. I hated Jaggar and everything he stood for, but I also knew how hard-headed my father could be. I wanted to ignore the idea that Jaggar was building an evil army of my peers. Yet, when he limped back to his chair by the fire, something in me broke a little.

We both waited in awkward silence. I knew he was waiting for me to say something, to explain myself, to thank him. But all the words stuck to my tongue. When I could think of nothing worthwhile to say, I bowed my head. Out of the corner of my eye, I saw him dip his head for just a moment. "I'm off to bed," he grunted as he rose. "We'll talk about this more in the morning." He looked at me with a profound mixture of emotions. There was pity and sorrow, but also guilt and shame.

I wanted to explain to him, to tell him exactly why I was stuck being precisely whom he didn't want me to be. But I couldn't. I didn't know myself. "Dad, I'm sorry—"

He held up his hand like a king asking for silence from his subordinates. Just like that, the conversation was over. I watched him limp through the doorway and into his bedroom. His bulky frame had to shift to get through the door built for mere men.

I balled my fists and closed my eyes. All the words I should have said were stuck in my throat. The fear and pressure from the day all hit me at once.

Jaggar's evil bidding, my father's odd maladies, and the knowledge that tomorrow I would have to face the world again, were all balanced on my shoulders.

Chapter Eight:

Mysteries In the Fog

The stairs that had called my name only moments before now seemed like a passage to a cage rather than my freedom. Anger burned in my chest, and tears brimmed in my eyes. I hung my satchel on a peg and groped blindly for the door in the darkness of the dying fire. When my hands finally found the handle, I slowly slipped off the lock. It made a soft *click* as the latch dropped. The rustling from the other room paused, and my heart froze. I exhaled a breath that seemed to rattle in my chest before finally escaping from my mouth as I opened the front door and slipped into the woods.

I ran into the growing darkness as a fog rolled in off of Odin's Ridge. It was the most enormous mountain located at the island's heart. Fog shrouded it at night and flooded the surrounding woods with mysteries. During the day, the mist rose up near the peak and solidified into clouds. The grass around me made soft, shushing noises as I ran through it. My dew-dampened pants were as heavy as my heart. The wind blew through my hair as I picked up speed. As I raced past, I caught clips of the nighttime bird's eerie tunes. I might have run forever if not for the rock hidden under a patch of wild linneas. My toe caught the stone, and I pitched headlong into the flowers. My fall beheaded several of the double-blossomed flowers, which then rained their pink and white petals down on me like snow. I wasn't severely hurt, but I didn't fancy getting back up, either. I didn't have a destination in mind, so why not here? I extended my oddly bent legs and groaned. Now that I wasn't moving, the air seemed to grow colder around me. I tucked one hand under my head and the other under my armpit for warmth.

What if I ran away and never came back? What if I constructed a life here in the woods? Made a castle of my own among the trees and ruled as a god over my domain? Would they care? Would they look for me?

I knew my life as a hermit in the woods would be short-lived. I had no way to hunt and no tools to build my home. Sooner or later, my father would drag me back into the world of people. Eventually, I needed to learn to act as if I liked it here. Take a seat on the council, maybe? No, I hated politics. I could join Birger as a partner in the workshop? No, I couldn't be tied down for very long.

A sigh escaped me. The overwhelming feeling seemed to echo from everywhere around me. A fog had begun to obscure my view of the trees above me. Slowly, everything was turning gray and miserable. Everything I saw only amplified the feeling. I didn't belong here. I didn't belong anywhere.

I sat up, and the fog wrapped around me like a blanket, sealing me in the frigid air. Shivering, I tried to stand up, but the linneas seemed to cling to me. My thoughts turned back to my father, and anger replaced my sorrow. That gave me the strength to fight off the flowers and finally stand. I buried my hands under my arms and hugged myself for warmth. *Just walk*, I told myself. *Maybe you'll find a place where he won't find you.* I kept my eyes glued to the ground, unwilling to trip again.

When I heard a little splash, my head jerked up. I was emerging from a fog and into a moonlit valley. Rock walls encompassed it on three sides. The one directly across from me had rocks jetting out of the water. From the looks of it, the water had drained recently. A low time in the month, most likely.

I tramped across the damp sands and towards the water. In the moonlight, it was a deep blue near the center and turquoise around the edges. I ran forward through the shin-deep water and towards the small opening.

I walked as far as I could while the tiny pebbles were dry. A rock wall surrounded the entire lagoon as if it had been cut from the mountain by a giant. I desperately wanted to see out over the water. I put a hand on the jagged edge of the wall and took a deep breath.

I climbed up the rock side a bit before looking out over the water. Each handhold brought me closer to the lip of the cliff. Shimmying over the edge and onto the flat top of the ridge left me breathless and a little shaky. I inched to the other side and peered down into the darkness. By the light of the moon, I could see the glittering ocean far below. The salty air rose on an ocean breeze and ruffled my curls into a frenzy. My heart began beating wildly as I gazed out over the waves. All of that open space just begging for me to come. The one place I had no fear of meeting people or confined spaces. It was perfect.

If only I could walk on water.

The stars glittered on the water's surface like lanterns on a velvet blanket. The moon illuminated a large portion of the otherwise inky sea, but I could see enough to make my heart yearn. I leaned into the wind, hoping to sail out there someday. If only I knew how to sail. If only boats weren't outlawed. I inhaled the scent of salt and adventure. I turned and sat down on the edge of the cliff overlooking the island. My tiny island in a sea of undiscovered places.

I closed my eyes and saw myself on a small watercraft in the open ocean. Surely the stars would shine even brighter without the lights of Eztenburg. I could practically hear the sound of the water lapping the side of my boat. What if there were unexplored islands out there? I wouldn't have to talk to anyone but the moon and the waves.

The vision disappeared like vapor when someone touched me. I didn't have time to whirl around or even scream before I fell. In that instant, my body became a live wire and I knew I had to seize the rock edge if I wanted to live. I grabbed the air, searching for something, *anything*, to stop gravity's pull. I was already falling. I knew rocks were waiting to smash me or impale me. I prayed silently, with no particular deity in mind. My only hope was that Birger wouldn't mourn for me too long and Jaggar wouldn't be overly pleased.

I braced for impact, awaiting the pain, only to be greeted with something much softer. The water met me, but I didn't sink or slap the surface of it. It rolled under me like a living tide. I kept my eyes squeezed shut for a moment longer.

I laughed. "I'm alive?" I opened my eyes hesitantly. I patted myself down to ensure I had all of my extremities. "I'm alive!" A giant wave was underneath me. That alone was enough to scare me to death. I turned to see everything more clearly. The massive wave bent and carefully moved me closer to shore.

I was set gently down in the ankle-deep water. "Thank you," I said to the pillar of water that stood above me. It cocked its head at me as if it were a dog. I did the same. It sprayed me, and I splashed back; it reared away as if it were not made of the same material.

I couldn't help but smile. "Hey, fella. What *are* you?" I held out my hand, almost like I was going to pet a timid animal. It fell back into the water around me. The ripples faded, and the waters stilled.

It was gone.

A quick glance at the cliffs confirmed that my attacker was too. I stared at the sight of the miracle I had just witnessed. I had lived on this island my whole life and never even knew this cove was here. I couldn't hold back the smile creeping onto my face. Sure, I had almost died, but how many people witnessed the sea moving of its own accord? With one last look over my shoulder, I turned back towards the mouth of the cove.

Chapter Nine:

The First Forsaken

The walk home was slow and perilous. I should have been watching where I was going, but that wouldn't have helped me.

My mind was elsewhere.

I was already forming theories and ideas about the odd creature that had just saved my life. What was that thing? Did it only dwell there in the pool? What would happen if all the water drained back into the ocean? Was it dangerous? Could it be tamed?

A resounding *thwap* and immediate pain broke my stupor. I yelped and rubbed my forehead, pulling the low-hanging branch I'd nearly knocked myself out on away from my face. With a hand slapped against my head, I looked around unsteadily. Because of the fog, I could only see a few steps in front of me at any given moment. I swatted the branch away and moved onward, but it hit me in the back once again.

Once the tree was a few paces behind me, it melted into the quiet nothingness that enveloped me. I was utterly at the mercy of the fog's twisting current. It always seemed to shift just enough to keep me from hitting another tree, but I was trapped in the swirling mist. I was vaguely aware that the trees had retreated when my porch swung at me through the haze. I tripped going up the stairs and landed on my knees on our front stoop.

How fitting, I thought bitterly, *that I should return to his domain on my knees.*

I rose, trying to scrape together what little dignity I had left. Hoping against hope that my fall hadn't awoken my father, I held my head high and eased the door open. I crawled up the stairs and into my bedroom leaving him none-the-wiser of my adventure.

Once the door was quietly closed behind me, I closed my eyes and breathed in the familiar scents that encompassed me. The friendly leather of my tool belt, the worn wool of my quilt, and wood smoke from the fire downstairs.

I moved to my desk and began tinkering with the many parts and tools I had perfectly scattered. I needed to sleep, but my mind seemed lost in the fog outside, trying to find its way back to that cove. Something tickled the back of my mind about that creature. There was an old story I had heard once about a strange creature who lived in the sea. The memory was connected to another; one of my mother.

I closed my eyes, letting myself get lost in the ghost of that day.

My father had elected to stay home with us to join in the fun. We played in the snow all day together, building snow forts, having snowball fights, and making snow people.

I vividly remember the snowball fight. It was my mother and me against my father. The walls of his snow fort were thick and high, while ours were already beginning to crumble. We were slumped behind our failing wall, snowballs flying over our heads. "What's the plan?" she whispered to me.

"I'll run out one way, and you run out the other. He can't take us both."

She smiled. "On three?"

I nodded.

"One, two, *three*."

We rushed to the fort at the perfect time. His back was to us as he scraped snow together to replenish his ammunition. My mother came around from the left, and I from the right. He laughed and threw a snowball at my mother. "Linnea!" he laughed, a giant grin growing under his beard.

She dodged and kept running at him, a similar smile on her face. He tackled her, and they rolled in the snow a fury of laughter and fresh powder. I watched and threw a pathetically timed snowball, which harmlessly hit a nearby tree.

My mother giggled as he kissed her forehead. I ran forward and threw my last snowball. It hit my father in the back, and he rolled over like he was dead. He groaned, closed his eyes, and stuck out his tongue for extra measure.

I jumped on him, and he sucked in a surprised breath. I sat up and tried to speak between laughs. "I have conquered this land!"

"What will you do with it, my king?" my mother said, sitting up herself.

"My first decree…" I trailed off, trying to think of what a good king might do.

"Get rid of the previous king!" my mother said with a laugh as she threw a handful of snow at my father. My father roared with laughter, scooped me up with one hand, and dusted off the snow from his face with the other. He laid back down, with me still wrapped in his arms and my mother leaning against his chest. We sat in the snow and gazed at the fading sun as it set behind Odin's Ridge.

My father pulled us closer as the fading sun took the heat with it. The warmth of his touch was enough to keep the cold off. We watched the sky change over the mountain until the stars winked at us. I shivered against the harsh air, and my mother scooped me up. My father swept her off her feet and carried us all into the house.

We changed out of our snow-caked clothes and into our warmest pajamas. The fire crackled in the hearth as I climbed into their bed. My father and I sat upright and expectant was she pulled an old book off the shelf and settled beside me. I snuggled in and grabbed the quilt, ready for an adventure. The snow fell softly in the inky blackness outside our window.

She smiled and began to sing softly.

Whether the sea be calm and clear tonight,

Or rough as the men's raging hearts.

My ship goes down to you tonight,

Oh god of wind and sea.

I opened my eyes. I had propped up my head under my arm and fallen asleep at my desk again. Wiping the sleep from my eyes, I stretched and waddled towards the bed. My chest ached, not from the stiffness of my uncomfortable nap at the desk. As much as I tried not to think about the wonderful memory I had just left behind, I couldn't help replaying it over and over.

I had almost forgotten about that romp in the snow. It had been so long ago. The memory was tainted with time, but it still carried the same emotions it had the day I witnessed it.

All weariness suddenly drained from me. It was like I had been doused in cold water. *The book.* The book she had read from that night. It was about the forsaken gods. I could picture the cover. It was worn thin and faded with age, but it had a sketch of a creature on the front. A creature made of water.

My heart began to race. The only problem was its current location. After my mother had passed, my father boxed up all of her old things and put them in the attic. Anything he didn't box up, he refused to move. The book was still on his bedside table under her wedding ring. Unlike the ring, it had layers of dust on it. We had no use for it, but he refused to move it from where she had last laid it. The question was, could I? Would I shake the dust from it, knowing it was probably the last thing she had touched?

Only one way to find out.

I shook my sleeping legs and crept towards the door, wondering how deeply my father really slept. When I opened the door, it squeaked loudly, shouting my intent to the whole house. Cringing, I waited for him to come to investigate. When nothing happened, I slunk down the stairs two at a time. The house was quiet. The coals shimmered in the fireplace. No light shone from under his door.

I pressed my ear against the door and waited. I closed my eyes, cupped my hands around my ear, and waited some more. I couldn't hear a thing; not a single breath escaped the room. The more I crouched there, the worse this idea sounded. I could have sworn he snored like a fog horn.

As I reached for the door handle, something squeaked outside. I froze in terror of being found out. After creeping back through the den and past the kitchen, I found the front door was slightly ajar. I peeked outside. The dark form of my father blocked out the moon. I waited, expecting something sinister. But nothing happened. His face was slightly lifted as if he were soaking in the moonlight. His feet rested on the stairs, but his arms were crossed. It was the most peaceful I had seen him in four years. The silence of the fog and the stillness of his body made me increasingly aware of each of my breaths and the little white puffs that leaked from my mouth into the night air.

I snuck back to his bedroom and opened the door, hoping the glow from the dying fire would illuminate my path. The room sucked in any light the dying coals or the moonlight let off. I took a deep breath and stepped inside, keeping my hands extended.

I felt the bedpost and the rumpled quilts. I made it to the second bedpost. I turned and began walking towards the head of the bed. My toe found the corner of the table. I slapped a hand over my mouth and sat heavily on the bed. I groaned and rubbed my toe to ensure it hadn't fallen off.

I slid my hand along the table and found the corner of the book. I tilted it until I heard the ring slide onto the top of the table. I hugged the book to my chest and scurried out the door again. As I closed the door behind me, I heard a floorboard squeak. I was flooded with panic and ran as quietly as I could to the stairs. Before I could make it up to my room, I saw my father outside.

He was walking up the stairs, clutching a flower. It split near the top and had two drooping flowers emerging from the split. He had tears in his eyes as he paused in the doorway. I clutched the banister as I crept up the stairs. He bowed his head as he entered the house and gingerly placed the flower on the windowsill. He lumbered past me, unaware or uncaring of my presence.

I began my rapid ascent up the stairs, but paused at the landing that my bedroom door was on, and I turned and gave one final look to the flower on the windowsill. It seemed to glow in the heavenly moonlight. That's when I recognized it.

There had been a time when our land was covered in those flowers. They spotted the countryside and dotted the horizon. Now, they barely survived the spring.

It was a linnea.

My throat constricted as I turned away and continued up the stairs. I only let a single tear fall when I reached my desk's safe haven. With one hand, I placed the book flat on my desk, with the other, I lit a candle. When the flame finally took to the wick, a pool of light overflowed onto the cover. A smile flickered across my face. Memory had served me correctly. The book had a faded sketch of an animated blob of water and a man looking up at it. I took a deep breath and held it for a moment. The title was:

THE VANIR

I opened it to the first page. There was no table of contents, just a warning in the middle of the page.

"The forsaken?" I whispered to myself, reading the inscription. A sudden gust of wind made my window panes rattle. I jumped, and my candle went out. I quickly relit it and swept the light around my room. I half expected a forgotten god's hulking figure to lurk nearby.

I was alone, so I turned the page and saw the words scribbled at the top:

ENTRY ONE: RAN. GODDESS OF FLOWING WATER.

The rest was marked out. I ran my fingers over it. My fingers came back dark and sooty. I rubbed some more. No matter how hard I rubbed, I could not uncover the words underneath. Beside the blob of dark, a few sentences were scribbled. The handwriting was none that I recognized:

EXTREMELY DANGEROUS. FORSAKEN IMMEDIATELY.

The next few pages were torn out. Fragments of the pages remained attached at the spine, but none of them had words I could decipher. The next entry was much the same:

GULLVEIG: EXTREMELY DANGEROUS. FORSAKEN IMMEDIATELY.

I flipped ahead again and read the names and descriptions under my breath.

FREYR: EXTREMELY DANGEROUS.

GERSEMI: FORSAKEN IMMEDIATELY.

VANA: EXTREMELY DANGEROUS.

HNOSS: FORSAKEN IMMEDIATELY.

Whole sections had been ripped out. The binding was ravaged and fragile. I turned the last page and found an entry written only in the smudged coal dust.

I read the next line to myself:

NJORD: GOD OF THE SEA. LITTLE IS KNOWN ABOUT HIM OTHER THAN HIS PARASITIC HABITS. HE

INFATUATES MEN WITH A LUST FOR ADVENTURE AND IDEAS OF WEALTH BEYOND THE HORIZON. HE LEADS THEM AWAY FROM THEIR FAMILIES, THEN DROWNS THEM.

HE IS THE FATHER AND LEADER OF THE VANIR. EXTREMELY DANGEROUS.

I skimmed through the next paragraph, terrified. It read:

IF GIVEN A CHANCE, RID THE WORLD OF THIS VILE AND WICKED GOD. THE ONLY WAY TO KILL HIM IS TO RID HIM OF HIS POWER SOURCE: THE SEA. HE WILL BE THE FIRST OF THE FORSAKEN.

I slammed the book shut, my heart pounding loud enough for even my father to hear downstairs. I had no memory of my mother reading me this. Abandoning the book and still burning candle, I scrambled to my bed. Some part of me whispered that a quilt would not protect me from anything, but it was better than nothing. I pictured a looming figure outside my window, his head bowed low in the darkness, his boney fingers raking across the panes. Dry lightning flashed and illuminated my assailant for a moment.

It was only a tree.

I laid back down and tried not to think about my encounter with a dangerous, murdering god.

Chapter Ten:

The Cove

Blearily, I opened my eyes only to be greeted by darkness. I reached up to wipe my eyes, and the quilt slid off my head. I sat up and ran my fingers through my hair. What time was it? It was still dark outside, but that didn't mean anything. I threw open a windowpane. The fog from last night hung oppressively low. No matter how hard the sun tried, it couldn't burn through the gloom.

I stumbled downstairs and found my father standing on the front steps with the door swung wide. The flower was gone. I eased behind him and watched him squint into the sky as if he could stare a hole in it.

"Somebody's got a secret," he grunted. "And a big one by the looks of it."

"What—what makes you say that?" I asked nervously as he passed me.

"The fog," he said as he lumbered through the doorway.

I sighed into the doorframe; maybe he didn't know after all. I closed the door. "You can speak water droplets and refracting light?"

"Sure do," he said as he took breakfast off the stove. He looked at me for the first time and paused. He cleared his throat and ran his fingers through his hair.

My face burned, and I turned away. I pushed my hand down onto my head and smashed my hair flatter. All I could do was hope it was a little better. He cleared his throat again in a nervous habit. "Breakfast?"

"Uh, no, actually. I think I'll go get dressed for work."

He choked on whatever he was sipping. "You're staying home today."

I paused on the stairs, a breath caught in my throat. Was this a punishment? Did he know more than he let on? Finally, I found my voice. "Any particular reason for that?"

"No," he looked suspiciously into his clay mug. "I'm just asking you… forcefully, to stay on our property. For the day."

"That's not... odd, or in the least bit concerning. May I ask why?"

"Just stay here. I thought that's what you liked. You just do… whatever it is you do."

"Wow, dad, thanks for summing that up for me. Not offensive in the slightest."

He took a deep breath and held it. "Right, well, I'm off. Counsel is deciding on *things*."

"Again? You had a meeting yesterday"

"Fickle things, people."

We shared a look. I could see a book of words he'd never said in his guarded gaze. Did he know how much I wished he would just pour them out on me like a fountain? *Apparently not*, I decided as his mouth became fixed and his gaze averted mine. "I have… things to do," I offered feebly as I jammed a thumb up the stairs.

He blinked hard. "Right. See you." Then he trudged out the door.

I blew out the huff I'd withheld, grabbed my bag, and shoved my journal and a new pencil into it. After casting an eye over my shoulder to make sure he was down the lane, I let the door close behind me and ran for the woods.

I stopped a few feet into the trees and pulled out a slip of paper.

Entered woods from the backdoor, I wrote.

I smiled, stuck the pencil behind my ear, and set off to find the cove again. Periodically, I would write two squiggles on a leaf of a low-hanging branch. Originally, I had debated carving something into a tree or just a slash with my knife, but those could be easily followed. Where I was going felt like a secret older than time. The charcoal would wash off in the next rain, and by then I would have the path memorized. So, my knife stayed in the bag. In this instance, the pen was much mightier than the sword.

As I walked, I kept careful notes of what I saw.

Passed gnarled tree.

Found a small pond, veered right.

Valley of flowers.

At the base of the mountain, turned right.

I wove between large rocks that had fallen from the eroding cliff edge. The small space would have made it impossible for a larger man to wiggle through. Had I really done all this last night without realizing it? I hopped over a rock and ducked under a log. The fog had still hung in ribbons throughout the forest, but there wasn't a trace of it here. There was the cove. The sun shone on the water and reflected back hues of orange among the blue and grays.

As I watched, a column of water rose from the surface. It bustled about and kept rushing towards the shore closest to the ocean, only to back off at the last second. I stepped forward to get a closer look. It saw me and charged the shore in one last effort but never mounted it. Angrily, it was repressed back into the depths from whence it came.

I ran forward, hoping to catch another glimpse of the creature, but it was gone. The water had receded a little more.

Was my imagination playing tricks on me, or were there more rocks at the mouth of the cove? It had been dark last night; perhaps I had assumed wrong.

I surveyed the water around the rocks and the sandy edges of the shore. There was no odd lump or pair of eyes glaring up at me. I was disappointed but not surprised. Gripping my bag tightly, I walked the perimeter of the little cove. A rock jutted out of the water only a little ways into the surf. It seemed like a good place to sit for a while. I took off my shoes and dipped my sore feet into the cold water. I waded over to the rock and sat down.

The cove was a beautiful place; I couldn't deny that. The trees above the overhang grew precariously over the edge. The roots were left twisted and grasping for straws over open air. Sparse grass grew in patches but the area was sand for the most part. Lots of small pebbles were mixed into the surrounding land. Vines hung from varying heights. The rocks around the edge were blanketed in moss and mushrooms.

The water moved and writhed like it was alive. For all I knew, it was. The water started light blue around the edge but began to ombre as the bottom dropped out near the middle. How deep did it go?

I retrieved my sketchbook and flipped to an open page while positioning myself with a clear view of the water and cliff edge. As I began drawing the creature and its surroundings, I got lost in the paper. I repeatedly paused and looked around, only to find once again that I was alone. I couldn't shake the feeling that I was being watched. Every time I turned around, I saw nothing, not even a ripple. Not long after that, I felt the sun being blocked out. A droplet of water fell and trickled down my forehead.

It was behind me.

Watching and possibly studying me, just as I was him. On impulse, I hunched my shoulders forward to hide my sketch and tried to fight the urge to run. I felt it shift when I did, move as I was. It was a strange sensation. I should have been terrified as the warning I read last night rang in my ears. Could I be the next victim in a long line of death-by-drowning victims? The creature behind me had a long and ugly track record, so a scrawny teenage boy would be easy for him to take down. I should have run screaming for the hills, but I could barely get myself to breathe. For once in my painfully short life, I felt no fear. Everything about the situation begged for panic, but I just took a few shaky breaths and waited. Whether I was waiting to die or waiting to live, I couldn't be sure.

I was immensely aware of the cool it radiated. Forgetting momentarily about the briskness of this morning, I almost enjoyed its proximity. I knew I'd feel its absence like the scorch of summer. When I finished the sketch, I held it to my side without turning around.

"What do you think?"

There was no answer, but I knew it was still there. There was a long silence during which I only watched its half-translucent shadow dance on me.

As I watched, the shadow slowly floated away. It passed me and brushed my rock so that water splashed me playfully. It continued towards the lake's center until it gradually sank into the water.

What had I done wrong?

Abruptly, a geyser erupted. Two jets of water squirted and danced along the water. The dance was intricate and well-choreographed. The water was alive and flitted about like a pit of snakes. It flowed like liquid lightning.

It waxed and waned like living ripples. *That's what I'll call you*, I thought. *Ripple, the maker of waves, keeper of shores, unknown guardian of all.*

Chapter Eleven:

Strange Tides

Once the waves calmed, he hovered above the water; he didn't turn away or run. This time, he held my gaze. I stood up and clapped, a massive grin on my face.

I could almost see him smiling as he sprayed me bashfully. I smiled and kept clapping as he bowed gracefully like a performer at the curtain fall. I laughed and went to sit back down, but my foot slipped on the slick rock. My heart seemed to jump into my throat as I threw out my arms to catch myself. Faster than lightning, he shot forward to grab me. Once he sat me down, he let go and sank back into the water a stone's throw away. His impromptu catch left my torso dripping with salt water, but for the moment, I didn't mind.

“Thank you,” I whispered. I rose to my knees to look him in the eyes. If he had eyes, that is.

If he was the monster everyone claimed, why had he helped me? That makes twice now. If he wanted me to drown, why not let me fall yesterday? If he meant me harm, why not let me fall?

He hovered still as if waiting for me to reject him. Despite the war raging in my mind, he was perfectly calm. If I imagined a face on the transparent mound, it would have huge eyes burrowing into mine. His mouth would have a gentle slope to it. His nose would be a giant, undefined blob.

Taking a deep breath, I pulled my leg out from under me. I slowly slipped a foot off of the rock. My toes barely skimmed the water, but already the water seemed to send a jolt through me. I hesitated before touching the water, waiting for him to react. I inhaled slowly through my nose and exhaled through my mouth, but I wasn't sure if it was to keep him calm or myself. Taking one more deep breath, I couldn't help but wonder if it would be my last. My foot slipped gingerly into the water, sending tiny ripples spread across the surface until they met the invisible curtain that animated the water before me.

Now both feet were on the sandy floor beneath the water. "Thank you." He didn't react, so I explained further. "For yesterday." I took another step forward. "You—you're incredible," I said, more to myself than him. Two steps from him, I paused. Would he attack like a cornered animal? Would he drown me as all the legends say? My heart beat wildly, but I fought to keep my breathing steady. To show him I meant no ill will, I extended my open hand, palm facing skyward.

He paused; so did I. We stood as still as the rocks growing moss all around us. My mind refused to stop swirling like the sand at my feet. We had abandoned him. If the book was to be trusted, then I was instructed to kill him, if that was even possible. We looked at each other, both full of fear and expectation—each waiting for the other to blink and scare the other away. I closed my eyes, waiting to drown or hear him plop into the water. Instead, I felt the cooling touch of the water's surface. It flowed around my hand. I could feel multiple currents, one that expanded like lungs, another that flowed like blood. Each was vital to its survival, and each flowed through my fingers.

I let out a breath I didn't know I was holding, and he backed away. We looked at each other for a long moment. He bowed low and sank into the water.

He was gone.

I was left alone, standing in frigid knee-high water. A smile I couldn't hold back stained my face. I splashed back through the water to grab my things. Once I had seized my sketchbook from the rock, I paddled the last few steps to the shore and began stuffing everything into my bag. Only when I was steps from the cave opening did I remember my shoes, which I had shoved into my bag. Hopping from one foot to the other on the pebbles, I took them out of my bag and stuffed my feet inside. I branded the experience into my mind, intending to write it all down at home.

I had work to do.

I bobbed and weaved my way through the rocks and trees. Already ideas were flashing through my mind. Tree branches swept low, trying to stop me. Rocks sprang up and tried to trip me. Nothing succeeded in slowing me down.

Finally, I reached the house. I came around the side of the house and ran up the steps onto our porch. I threw open the door, not caring how loud it was banging closed. I was alone, after all. I ran across the den and raced up the stairs.

"Hello, Kam."

I jumped so hard my foot slipped on the stairs and I slid back down them. My rump ached, but I composed myself and stood up, rubbing my new bruises. Peering over the rail, I searched for the ghost that had spoken my name. At first, I didn't see anyone. Leaning farther over the rail, I called, "Birger?"

Then I saw him in the kitchen. "What've you been up to?" He asked as he toddled around the kitchen doing gods-know-what.

"I've—" I started to gush about my day, then caught myself. "What are you doing here?" I walked down a few more stairs to see him more clearly.

He smiled as he walked over to meet me. "Your father sent me over to watch you." I was almost his height from my position at the foot of the stairs. Just to see if I could be taller than him, I stood on my tip-toes and braced myself on the rail. His bushy eyebrows raised as I miraculously grew. I sank back to my normal height and jumped to the floor.

"I always did need a babysitter," I said glumly.

"Aye, but I'll stay out of your business." He returned to the kitchen to prove he was true to his word.

I walked back up the stairs slowly. I trusted Birger with everything, but could I trust him with this? I hesitated at my door. No, I decided. I would let this play out and allow cards to fall as they may. There would probably come a time in the not-so-distant future when I got in over my head and needed his help. But until that time came, I would guard Rip's secret.

I closed the door behind me and set to work. I grabbed my tool belt and some materials.

I ran back down the stairs. “Hey, Birger?” I called.

“Here!”

I rounded the corner to find him making a tremendous sandwich out of anything and everything we had in our kitchen.

“Oh my—is that *eel*? On a sandwich?”

“Yes, want some?”

“Think I’ll pass. Could I go… get some materials?”

“Why? What are you building?”

“Actually, I need to fix something.”

“Where are you going? Not far, I hope.”

“Nope, should be back really fast.”

“I'll be up in a bit. To watch. Going to eat this first.” He ripped a chunk out of his sandwich and threw it into the fire. The smell of burning fish filled the room

“Take all the time you need,” I coughed. Eel could kill anyone’s stomach, so I didn’t think he would be coming anytime soon. As I strolled into town, I kept a sharp eye out for my father. I didn’t know who else he’d told about my strange confinement. I didn’t want him to ask any unnecessary questions. The one person I didn’t expect to see was the one person who saw me.

Rowan came up beside me. “Where are you going?” he asked.

“Work.”

“I thought it was closed today.”

“Is it? It is,” I stammered. “Just me today,”

“Everyone’s going to the council meeting.”

"That's… a first."

"So where are you going?"

"To grab something."

"Sure. What are we voting on today?" He narrowed his eyes suspiciously and opened his mouth to accuse me of something.

"Uh… oh, look, I'm here." I began frantically reaching for the knob. It was locked. I fumbled behind the shutter for the spare key Birger kept hidden. "It was nice seeing you. Thanks for the chat." I offered a feeble wave as I slammed the door closed. I put my back against the door and waited, confident I could feel his stare borrowing a hole through the door. Finally, I heard him softly pad away.

I walked to the furnace and got the fire started. Then, I opened the window at my desk and carefully laid out my supplies. As the fire burned hotter, I hammered leather and set screws. I poured liquid glass, molded hot metal, and braided metal wires before sealing them with sap. I pushed and lugged and sweated. Only when the low sun was streaming in through the window. I plunged the fiery metal into a bucket of ice-like water and watched the stream rise with great satisfaction.

I pushed the glass-rimmed goggles over my head and eyes. I tightened the straps and looked around the room. Everything was blurry and unclear, but I could see. I put the metal pacifier in my mouth, blew out a gust of air, and heard it push out the other end. I took a breath, and air came back through the pipe. Casting a glance to the open window, I took off everything before anyone could walk in on me. I would look bug-eyed and crazy. Well, more so than usual.

I stuffed it all carefully into the apron and walked home. Tomorrow, Rip wouldn't know what hit him.

Chapter Twelve:

House Arrest

I walked in the door to find Birger passed out on a chair. His head rested on his large chest and his legs were sprawled in front of him. I snuck carefully up the stairs, hoping we were alone. The new inventions in my bag seemed illegal to have. Carefully so no one would hear me, I stowed the bag under my desk. What if someone found it? What if they started asking questions? How would I explain my behavior? How would I protect Rip?

I jumped when the front door banged shut. Someone called out, but I couldn't make out the words. Sneaking to the door, I inched it open to eavesdrop. After closing the door softly behind me, I tiptoed down a few stairs to peer through the gaps in the rail. My father turned and saw Birger asleep where I'd left him. "Birger," he said. "Bo!" he shouted. A snore erupted out of Birger, and I barely kept from laughing. He shook Birger's shoulder until his eyes opened. I pressed my face to the bars and gripped the rail as I squatted silently on the top stair.

"Where is he?" my father asked.

Birger was still a little dazed, "Upstairs. Hasn't come down since you left."

"Good." I heard him sit down. "I don't want him around anyone right now."

There was an awkward moment of silence. I watched the memory of our last conversation dawn on Birger's face. He flushed and wrung his large hands. "He did go get something a while ago," Birger confessed.

"What did he get?"

"Supplies."

"For what?"

"I—I'm not sure."

"How long was he gone?"

I heard the change in Birger's voice. He realized he didn't know if I was back at all. "I don't know," he admitted quietly.

"How long has he been back?"

"He—" Birger paused. "I couldn't tell you."

With a grunt, my father stood up suddenly. "Kameron!" I heard him marching towards the stairs. How suspicious would I look, eavesdropping from the top of the stairs? I'd look guilty. Like I was hiding something. I had to move.

I jumped up, but tripped and tumbled down a few before I caught myself on the rail. Once I had stopped rolling, I looked up and found him leaning against the railing, looking down at me. I offered him a weak smile. “Hiya, dad,” I offered feebly.

He raised his eyebrow, and I saw his jaw clench under his beard. “Dad,” I breathed as I sat up. He looked worse than I felt. Sure, my shoulder hurt, and my hip would have an Odin’s Ridge sized bruise on it tomorrow, but he looked lucky to be standing. The left side of his face was bruised green and purple. One eye was swollen nearly shut. He favored a leg, and his knuckles dripped blood down his fingers and onto the old wood boards.

He ignored me and put his hands on his hips. “Why’d you leave?”

I began trying to stand up, but I was twisted into a strange position, and the uneven floor wasn’t helping much.. “I needed to grab something.”

“D’ya talk to anyone?”

"Does myself count?"

I saw Birger smile, but my father didn't look amused. "You're grounded, young man."

I finally managed to get my feet under me but staggered at that news and grabbed the rail to keep myself upright. "What? Why?"

He looked desperately around the room. "For—for this." He picked me up by my shirt. "It's filthy. That's a week of house arrest."

"I was working, dad; I didn't have time to change." I tried to keep the exasperation out of my tone but failed miserably.

"How long have you been home?"

"A little bit," I said, keeping my eyes down. I rounded the end of the rail and jumped down the last stair to stand even with him.

"Lying too! That's two weeks."

My mind spun in circles. Had he found out about Rip? What had he done to him? "Dad, please, I can explain. I don't know how you found out, but just give me a chance to defend—"

His large, blood-stained hand lifted, and I ducked. "Upstairs." I looked up to find him pointing up the stairs. My gaze flickered from the grotesque hand to his face, then to Birger. Birger looked baffled and concerned all at once but he still wouldn't meet my eyes.

My face smoldered. I stomped up the stairs as forcefully as possible, but I couldn't even rattle the dust motes. I threw a scalding glare back down the stairs, but my father was gone before I reached my door. I grabbed the handle and swung the door open but didn't step through. I closed it loud enough for them to hear, then sat on the top step.

It wasn't half a second later that the explanations began pouring from his mouth like a fountain. That was his one fatal flaw. He felt he owed everyone a reason for everything. It was as if he witnessed the crime and needed to be sure the jury understood the injustice of it all.

"You can't keep him here forever. He's going to get out there again. He has a way of sneaking around, you know. So small, meek, easy to overlook. He might be sneaking out now," Birger said.

"I know, but I just want to keep him here… as long as I can."

Anger boiled in me, dangerously close to exploding. He always had to have the last word. I stood silently, hands balled into fists, unwilling to hear the rest. Whatever the counsel had decided, it hadn't ruled in my favor. No matter what happened to me, it wouldn't be my decision.

I entered my bedroom and began throwing things in my bag for tomorrow. Everything I'd made in the shop, some food, a water flask, a map I had begun cartographing. And, of course, my sketchbook. I sat on the stool in front of my desk, trying to clear my head. What would my father do if he knew I was breaking the law? Was this even illegal? I thought back over the day yesterday. The strength of his dance. The quiet power of his presence. I'd never met a god, but I didn't think anyone else could fit the bill better than Ripple.

I fumbled for a pencil and began jotting down my trip's highlights. I didn't want to forget a single moment. I wrote about how I'd found his cove, how his water had felt as it flowed through me, seeing him rise from the watery depths for the first time. But most of all: the hope of seeing him soon.

Before long, I heard footsteps coming up my stairs. They weren't the usual *stomp-stomp-stomp*, which meant I had done something awful and was about to be scolded and called a disappointment. It always ended with both of us feeling belittled and angry.

These were a quiet *step-step-step*. Someone rapped on my door with two knuckles. “Kam? May I come in?”

“Er, sure?”

It was Birger. He opened the door and closed it gently behind him. Completely unlike my father, who tended to barge in unannounced. “I forgot to come up here earlier… and I’m going to leave in a minute. So, what have you been working on?”

“Oh, uh..” I raked all of my sized and scaled templates and the notes I’d done into a pile on the opposite side of my desk. I kicked my bag with the invention farther under my desk. “I wouldn’t necessarily say I *made* something. I just got stuff for when I did. Er—if, *if* I did.”

"Oh, very clever of you." He absentmindedly cranked the lever on the side of my pencil sharpener. We both stared at the lever and listened intently to the gears grinding. "Your father means well."

My heart seemed to skip a beat. Why couldn't we just sit in silence? "I know," I whispered.

"He just doesn't quite know how to tell ya."

I remembered the anger I'd felt earlier, then the dream I'd had last night. "Birger, can I be honest for a second?"

He sat on the edge of my bed and gave me a small smile. I turned slightly on my stool to face him. The whole bed was raised to compensate for the sudden weight at the end. "Go ahead."

I looked away. "Sometimes," I paused, already hating myself for admitting it, "I wish *you* were my dad."

I knew his expression would be a mix of shock and anger, so I didn't look. I heard him get up. Instead of rough hands grabbing my shoulders, his calloused hands wrapped around me. He pressed my head against his large stomach. His steady hands held me as I breathed in his musk. He drew back and knelt down to look at me. I averted my eyes. His large hand gently lifted my chin to look at him.

"Your father loves you very much, and I know you love him too. You are a Kovah. And with that title comes a hindrance for spoken words, apparently. Maybe if you open up a little, he'll do the same. You get what you give."

He gave me a smile.

I tried to mirror it.

"Birger!" my father yelled, he sounded slightly panicked.

"Your old man needs my help again." Birger stood to leave.

I looked away, trying not to let him see the mix of emotions rising in me. "Woah there, if he hears you call him old you might lose your head," I said halfheartedly, rubbing the back of my neck to hide the rising heat in my face.

He chuckled and ran his thumb across his throat.

"Today, Birger!" my father called.

"I'm done for," Birger sighed.

I chuckled.

His fierce eyes softened a moment. He bent down and gave me a big hug. "I won't be seeing you in the shop for a while, but if you need more materials," he affectionately thumped me on the back, "give me a hollar."

I stretched my shoulders. He'd nearly launched me across the room. "Alright, I will."

He opened the door and descended the stairs. My mind raced. I ran to the door to see him go. “Bye!” I yelled down to him. He paused on the landing and gave me a wave.

Chapter Thirteen:

Conversations In the Dark

I hesitated in the open doorway. Should I? Should I even try to voice my worries or fears to him? Would he even listen? Would he reciprocate the chance?

I looked out of the window and saw Birger's outline in the fading light. I steeled myself and grabbed the door handle.

For Birger.

I paused on the top step, one hand still on the door handle in case I needed to retreat into the safety of my room. "Hey, dad?"

"Aye?"

"Could we… have a word?"

“Sure, sure.” I heard him clear his throat as if silencing someone.

I quietly descended the stairs and entered his darkened dominion. Hushed voices flowed from the main room. As I rounded the banister, I saw why. Three dark forms reclined at the table. “I didn’t realize we had company.” I began backing towards the stairs again. “I’ll just wait. It’s unimportant—”

“No, Kameron, join us.” It wasn’t a question, and this time it wasn’t my father that addressed me. It was Jaggar. He sat between Birger and my father, a platter of untouched food in front of them. I walked forward tenderly, afraid of moving too fast. I stood silently at the edge of their group. The idea of going further appalled me.

“Jaggar and I were just discussing… business.”

“Yes,” Jaggar agreed after a glance at my father, “business.” His voice was slick as a snake and sharp as a tack. The fact that he now sat in my house would haunt my dreams.

My eyes shifted to the third form. Birger was still here. He sat quietly, assessing the situation. Wine glasses sat in front of each of them, all dusty and unused. A charcuterie board of food sat in front of them as well. The only parts missing were the parts I smelled burning in the fire.

“Well,” I said, trying to keep my voice from shaking. “Don’t let me kill the conversation.”

“Actually,” Jaggar hissed, “we were just discussing you.”

“Oh,” a nervous laugh escaped me. “That does kind of kill the gossip, doesn’t it?”

Jaggar eyed me suspiciously. “You and your father are… close, yes?”

My father opened his mouth, but I spoke quickly. "You could say that," I stammered.

"And you like working for him?" he thrust his thumb at Birger.

"Yes," I said indignantly. "Birger is the best boss ever."

"Interesting," Jaggar breathed.

"What's so important that you had to come all the way down here to discuss it?"

Jaggar looked confused. My father gave me a glare.

"Why couldn't you have waited for my father to get to city hall in the morning."

"Oh, this isn't that kind of business."

"So this is a personal call?"

Jaggar recovered quickly. "I suppose so."

I straightened and walked over to the untouched wine bottle. My father reached to help me, but I protested. It was opened already, which was excellent for me; I could have never opened it alone. I picked up each of their cups in turn and filled them halfway. When I reached Jaggar, I paused. Jaggar meant to cause trouble, that much I knew. He met my eye and seemed to pierce me with his glare. Rowan and his dad had one key difference despite all the other similarities. Jaggar's eyes were cold, like the sea after the storm; Rowan's held lightning. I picked up his glass to fill and poured myself a cup as well.

Jaggar raised his glass towards my father, then to me. A small smile spread across his thin lips. "To your health."

They all drained their cups, but I stood mute as dread settled on my body. Something felt wrong. "Well, I should be off. Lots of important… things to do."

"Didn't you want to talk?"

Birger gave me a hopeful look, but I didn't meet his gaze. "It can wait."

I turned to hurry up the stairs but paused as the curtain shifted in the soft wind, and I caught sight of the moon outside. It looked like the moon had drunk the rest of our wine. The moon was full and hung oppressively low over the ridge; its light was blood red rather than its usual welcoming hue.

"Something wrong?" Jaggar's icy voice cut through the spell cast by this magic moon, and I hurried back up the stairs and closed the door behind me as quietly as I could. Voices resumed immediately downstairs. At times, the noise swelled into shouts. I remained holed up in my room, trying unsuccessfully to block out everything. Finally, I just sat down in front of the door, my back pushing against the wood grain as if that could keep out the noise. An ensuing crash from downstairs made me nearly jump out of my skin. The front door slammed, and I heaved a sigh. That had to be Jaggar.

Not long after, the argument resumed, but this heated discussion died out quickly. I remained braced against the door, waiting for someone to come beat it down. The front door shut again, but quietly this time. That would be Birger. That meant it was just my father and me in the house again.

I took a deep breath and inched open my door. One uncertain step out the door left me trembling on the top step listening to the muttering rising from downstairs. The room was dark without the sunlight pouring in, so as I peered over the side of the rail, I had to squint through the gloom. He was cleaning up the table and grumbling to himself. His back was to me. I quietly descended the stairs. He didn't acknowledge me, but he knew I was there. I waited at the bottom of the stairs, hoping he would say something. *Anything*.

I cleared my throat of my stutter. “How was the meeting?”

I stood awkwardly behind him. He faced the fire. His voice was gravelly and rough. “Fine, fine.”

“What was it about?”

“Planning.”

“For…?”

“Crop rotations.”

“I thought that was up to—”

“The army, son!” He turned around suddenly. His eyes were red and swollen. He leaned on the counter heavily

“What happened?”

“A disagreement.”

“I’m not blind. Jaggar did this? Just now?”

He looked at me for a long moment, then dropped his eyes and nodded.

"But… you never lose a fight."

He glanced my way and looked away quickly.

"You didn't even try," I said mostly to myself. My voice quivered. "What did you decide?"

He stood and began to pace. "You heard me. At the picnic. We're going to raid houses," he made no effort to conceal the tracks of his frustrated tears. "Those sheep-minded fools are willing to send their children into his company just for money and *preservation*!" He spit the last word like venom and stroked his graying beard.

"Who?" I asked quietly as I sat on the corner of the table.

"No amount of pleading or reading of Eztenburg's Book will change his mind."

"*His*? This is all Jaggar?"

"Aye, all of the council is in the palm of his hand. He tried blackmailing me into his graces." He hobbled over to a cabinet and pulled papers out from a compartment. He's tried paying me." He produced a bag that jingled when it thunked on the table. "He wanted to humiliate me out of the council." He sat down at the table and put his head in his hands. "He's tried peace, violence, words, laws, everything. Just to get me on *his* counsel." He turned to me and held my shoulders gently. "He's stooped low enough to threaten you."

I saw the fear in his eyes where there had never been before. "What's going to happen?" I asked quietly.

He pressed my head into his chest and held me a moment. I could hear his heart beating as hard as mine was. I could smell the disastrous dinner he'd shared with Jaggar. He pulled away and ran a hand across his forehead. "They told me you were dead."

"He what?" I straightened.

"He told me he sent men to the house, that they—" he took a shuddering breath. "He said they did awful things to you. He wouldn't let me out of his sight, so I sent Birger to check on you." A small smile crept over his words. "There you stood. Right as rain."

"That's why you don't want me to leave the house? You think I'm going to get mugged?"

He nodded and sank into his chair.

My heart beat faster. What if those men had come and I wasn't here? Would they have hurt Birger? What would happen when Birger finally realized how stubborn my dad was? I sat on the floor in front of him, forcing him to look at me. "How long do you think this can last, dad? How long can he keep you in fear? How long until he pulls something?" I paused. He raised his eyes to meet mine. "How long until you expose him?"

"I—I don't know."

"Well, what are we going to do about this?"

There was a long pause. He looked to the door as if imagining Jaggar was standing just beyond it. For all I knew he was. "I'm going to join his counsel."

I stood up, an icy dose of fear running down my back. "No, dad, that's exactly what he wants! You can't give in, he'll run all of Eztenburg."

"What's the other choice?"

"You say no!"

"And risk you?" He shook his head. "No."

"I'm fine, I will be fine. But you can't just let him—"

He stood up too fast, I stumbled back. "I said no!" He thrust a finger at my bedroom door. "Upstairs." When I flinched but didn't move, he lowered his voice and growled, "Now!"

I picked myself up, any shred of respect I had in his eyes was gone. We shared a knowing look before I turned away and trudged up the stairs. I closed the door and turned the latch to lock it. Leaning my head against the door, I could see straight down to the crack under the door. My shadow was stark compared to the darkness just outside my door.

How could I have been so blind? Of course Jaggar was blackmailing my father! He probably paid Rowan to torture me at work every day. I closed my eyes and imagined Jaggar describing in horrific detail how I begged for his son to stop, to leave me alone, how I whimpered and bled to my father, who only bowed his head in silence.

The restrained anger I'd held back far too long came boiling to the surface. Slamming my hand against the door, I turned and threw open my window.

I felt a sob welling up in my chest, a scream for help I'd held in far too long. I balled my fist and slammed it into the windowsill. Why couldn't he see that this was his one chance to dethrone Jaggar? Why couldn't he take it? I sagged onto the window and rested my chin on my arms. My knees hit the floor, and I sat awkwardly, looking out of the window at the moon.

The moon was so big tonight. It hung low on the horizon, brushing the branches of the trees. It blanketed all of the island in its red mystery. I hoped that somewhere out there in the great wide world, there was someone who had never heard of my measly little island. They could live a happy little life far away from the treacherous people that haunted my home. And just maybe we were looking at the same blood-soaked moon.

How could someplace, ordinarily so beautiful, be inhabited by such habitually evil people? The stars twinkled overhead. The crickets sang nearby. The mountains folded into gently rolling hills. Smoke rose from a hundred chimneys. The waves crashed on the East facing cliffs.

People plotted in the shadows. Bribe money exchanged hands. Threats leaked out of their lips. Even so, the Eden around them grew that much more beautiful.

Chapter Fourteen:

Swimming Techniques

Early the next morning, I was off. I didn't see my father before I left, and didn't plan on speaking with him anytime soon.

Sleep had evaded me most of the night. To bide my time, I poured over my notes and planned my day. As I marched into the woods, I went over the steps that were ingrained in my memory.

Enter the woods through the back door.

Pass the gnarled tree.

Turn right at the small pond.

Walk through the valley of flowers.

Turn right at the mountain.

Enter from the cleft in the rock.

Pause at the log.

I took a deep breath and peered around the fallen tree. It had tumbled from the clifftop at some point in the distant past and lodged diagonally in the gap of stone. Moss blanketed the underside, and mushrooms peppered the sides.

I peered around the tree and into the cove. Birdsong echoed through the bowl of stone. The surface of the water glittered invitingly. Nothing moved except the occasional breeze rippling through the trees above me. There were definitely more rocks at the mouth of the cove. From my perch here, I could barely see the ocean. I side-stepped the log and entered the glade. The wind whistled hollowly through the trees and over the ridge above me. It was as though time had stopped in this place. The rest of the world could go on without me; I was content to hide away here forever. Centuries could trickle by unnoticed. This was the only place not tainted by the stench of man.

I put all my things down on the pebbles far from the water's edge. Still panting from my hike, I knelt to unpack my goggles and breathing contraption. Fingering the thin tube I was about to stake my life on, I had a split second of doubt. Was I really about to climb into the water knowing full and well there was a monster hidden under the waves?

Half of me looked at the water, and fear threatened to overtake me, but the other half whispered of hope. What made this creature a monster? He could be just as lost and confused as I was. With that in mind, I knelt to remove my shoes, socks, and shirt. Now just in my pants, which I rolled up to avoid snagging, I slid my goggles over my head and tightened the straps accordingly. After a quick glance around to ensure I was alone, I slipped the tube in my mouth and looped the long cord around my arm. Then I removed the sliver of a broken mirror I had brought. Here, I had no fear of judgment except for the birds.

I assessed the situation dryly. I still looked mostly sane with the goggles on my head, but once they fit over my eyes, I was crazy looking. More so than usual. My eyes appeared three times as large as they should be, like an insect or a strange fish. The metal breathing tube vaguely resembled a fish hook, and the long rope could be the line. Overall, I resembled an oversized fish an unfortunate fisherman had hooked.

I looked around nervously, praying to whichever god would listen that no one would see. If only I were that lucky. A gurgling noise that resembled a laugh resounded from the water. Ripple was staring at me, or he would be if he had eyes. I quickly took off the goggles.

"I know, I know," I said. "But what would you expect me to do?"

Rip moved backward a step.

"I don't know what's in that water! I—I could go blind." He moved back again. He and I both knew I wasn't afraid of the water but of the creature inside it. I gripped the goggles in one hand and headed toward the shore. I found a large piece of driftwood that I hoped would float, then gently tied the tube around it. Tight enough to stay but loose enough to let air through the hollow part.

I gripped the other end with my teeth, nervously chewing the rubber end. I dipped a toe in the cool water. It was already lower than yesterday. The sun had warmed the lesser water, so it was warmer than ever. But once the surface reached the bare skin of my chest, it felt just as cold as it had before.

Ripple cocked his head again, watching my entry in mild fascination. I pulled down my goggles and took a huge breath. Thrusting my head underwater, I squeezed my eyes shut, heart throbbing, lungs already yearning for air. When my goggles didn't fill with water, I braved a look at the blue underworld. Although I was still in shallow water, it was a fantastic experience. Seaweed waved and danced in the rippling sunlight. Sand swished along the bottom with the small currents. Crabs darted into their holes as I swam overhead. My lungs struggled at first, still thinking there was no available air. I gulped air from my pipe and got a nose full of water.

I breached the surface like a whale and gasped for breath. My nose burned from the salty water, but I was determined to beat this learning curve. This time, I held my nose as I dove down. When I took a breath, my nose tried to help, but I pinched harder to keep water from sucking into my brain. I tended to swim in circles with only one arm, but a solution to that was already forming in my brain.

I took a huge breath and let the pipe slip from my mouth. It stayed near the top since it was tied to the log as I dove deeper into the blue until my ears popped. I felt something brush past me like a warm breeze. It was hard to distinguish Ripple from the rest of the water, but he was certainly there. When he flitted over seaweed, it parted. When he barreled through schools of minnow, they scattered.

I had no idea how long he had been here, but he had undoubtedly outgrown his lagoon. My lungs burned, reminding me I was *not* a fish, so I let go of my nose and swam upwards. Abruptly, my whole body was encompassed in warm water. I shot upward like an arrow. Ripple never lost contact with the water, but I catapulted into the open air. The view would have taken my breath away if I hadn't been trying to regain it. I slapped the water moments after sucking in a huge breath. I kicked until I was sputtering on the surface of the water again. I paddled and kicked to tread water. Eventually, I worked it into a rhythm. I pushed my goggles onto my forehead and smiled. That hadn't been so bad after all.

Rip bulged above me as if he was ensuring my safety. He radiated power; I could almost feel it like a tangible thing pulsing around him. My breath shook as I craned my neck to look up at him. He contained the power of great help or great destruction, yet I still chose to be this close to him. We looked at each other a moment before he shot a gentle geyser of water at me. Just like that, the moment of awe passed, and he seemed to shrink. I dipped my mouth under and spit water at him as well. He dodged and hit me with a shower of water drops again. I laughed and splashed him. He came closer and hovered above me. He slowly sank into the water until he melded with the shape of my head and eased the goggles off of my forehead.

I grabbed for them. “Hey, I need those!” Ignoring me, he spat them out, and we watched them splash into the deepest part of the pool. “You’re hilarious; you know that?” I couldn’t keep swimming now, I wouldn’t be able to see. Somewhat disheartened, I began swimming to the edge. I expected him to react somehow, but he didn’t. He watched me somberly as my feet brushed the soft sand of the shallows. Pausing to look at him, I couldn’t help but notice the sadness in his posture, in his silence. I looked down at the water again, then back at my abandoned things on the shore. What did I have to rush home to? A day of isolation.

I had come this far. Why leave because of a playful joke? How hard could swimming without them be?

"I guess I have a little while longer," I admitted, kicking off the bottom and swimming in his direction. He bobbled excitedly and swept me up playfully, dumping me deeper into the pool. He disappeared under the waves, obviously wanting me to follow him. I hesitated before diving after him, feeling the water course around me. I didn't have my goggles, and my breathing tube drifted closer to shore. After weighing my options, I took a deep breath and dove under to meet Rip.

I opened my eyes and marveled at the new world around me. The goggles had distorted and skewed the scenery. Now, the watery depths were brand new for exploring. If I concentrated, I could see the outline of Ripple zooming around me. Despite my best efforts, I couldn't keep up with him. He did a loop around me, spinning me in a quick circle. I laughed, causing a burst of bubbles to explode out of my mouth, then swam back up to the surface, racing my own bubbles as I dashed upward. Pushing the hair from my eyes, I gulped a salty breath before driving back down. I swam until my hands brushed the sand into little tornadoes. Warm water rushed past me as Ripple grabbed a bundle of seaweed and plopped it on my head. I smiled and flipped it over my shoulder. I had watched girls do the same thing while flirting with other boys in town.

He darted around wildly. I tried to stay down as long as I could, but when my burning lungs threatened to smother me, I couldn't ignore the pain. I put two feet on the ground and pushed. I flew upwards until my head breached the water. Rip met me just as I was slinging the hair from my eyes. "Sorry, Rip, I can't hold my breath that long," I said between breaths. He cocked his head sideways again. "I'll get better, though, with practice."

He ducked under again, but I kept treading water this time, trying to catch my breath. I gulped air and paddled to where the tube floated. I put it in my mouth and blew hard. Water shot out of the other end. *Good,* I thought. *Now I won't suck up the water.* I took a hesitant breath through the tube to test that thought. Water didn't fill my lungs. I didn't drown. I took a deep breath and dove down. I didn't see Ripple, so I kept swimming deeper. When I tried to breathe, I got a short puff of air before I gulped water. I saw the other side of the pipe sinking beside me. Uselessly, I spat out my end and coughed and gagged under the water, creating a flurry of bubbles. My arms and legs kicked sporadically, trying to propel me upward.

When my fingertips were about to brush the surface, something wrapped around my foot. I glanced down. I couldn't see anything in the gathering darkness but water, so it must be Ripple. Involuntarily, I gasped but only got water. He jerked me farther under the water and into the deepest part of the cove. I saw something glint from the corner of my eye, but I had more pressing issues. Above me, the surface glittered invitingly, but no matter how hard I struggled, I couldn't reach it. The water around me kept pushing me back down.

Every square inch of water seemed to be pressing in on me. I could hear my heart beating in my ears. Could that be because it was about to stop forever? My lungs felt like they were on fire. I burned for air, and I burned with hatred. But not for Rip.

This was my own fault.

Why had I ever thought this was a good idea? Why did I think this creature was my friend? I kicked and fought, but the grip on my foot never wavered. I was going to die down here; that thought settled on me like a load of bricks.

Balter's Ballad had tried to warn me of this. My mother's book had told me precisely that this would happen.

My lungs burned from the lack of oxygen. I dimly saw Rip's face in front of me. I wanted to push him away, but he was much faster than I was. As the last bubbles slipped from my mouth and my conscience was fading, I felt something tickling my nose. Unintentionally, I sucked in a breath. Water streamed into my lungs, but this time it didn't send sharp pains through my chest. I coughed and sputtered as life rushed back into me, but I only inhaled more. I could taste the air despite being hopelessly far from the surface.

Without warning, we were zooming back towards the surface. Once again, Rip scooped me up and placed me gingerly on the ground. At first, I was only vaguely aware of the sand beneath my fingers. Then I felt water beading down my face. Water ran back up my throat. I rolled over and began to gag up some of the water I had swallowed. I coughed until my sides ached. My lungs burned, but the air had never tasted sweeter. Shudders ran through my body as I laid back on the sand, feeling the sun on my skin. I could still feel water pressing down on me. My breath caught in my throat as I thought of all that water still sloshing around in my lungs.

My stomach tied itself into knots. My chest ached. My hands shook as I tried to wipe the hair from my eyes. I repeatedly swiped at the water on me but couldn't seem to get it off me. When I opened my eyes, the world seemed to spin around me.

Once I felt I could speak again, I rolled onto my back and stared up at him. I inched back a couple more inches from the surf.

"What was that for?" My voice was raspy and thin.

He only stared at me.

"You tried to drown me!" My voice threatened to give out from the strain of trying to breathe and talk at the same time.

He gestured back towards the water.

"I thought we were pals, or at least heading that direction!"

He took a step back and nodded at the water.

"Have you heard a single thing I've said?"

He shook his head.

"Ugh," I sat up and put my head in my hands.

One of my feet was on the surf's edge, and he prodded it. I jerked it back and sat cross-legged, glaring at him.

He cocked his head. He would have been begging me to join him again if he could speak.

"Why would I? So you can finish the job?"

I closed my eyes only to be flooded with images of being dragged up to the water's surface. Rip had carefully placed me back on the sand. *He* had been the one to drag me up from the bottom of the cove. My skin itched from the suffocating feeling of being enclosed on all sides. I opened my eyes to ask him more questions, but he had disappeared back into the depths.

I stood up warily, legs trembling. Why did the water seem to call to me? Had it really been only a few minutes ago that I feared for my life? I stepped back into the water slowly. It felt different, somehow. As if it met my skin with less resistance. There was no better feeling in the world. I tried to keep the smile off my face. When I was waist-high, I dove in headfirst. I resurfaced to find Ripple staring at me.

“So what was that really about?” My voice was stronger, somehow, like the water had empowered me.

He looked down at the water before going down. Hesitantly, I dove under as well. He met me halfway down, and we shared a look. He descended farther, so I had to follow him. He frolicked, and I barely managed to keep up. I waited for the familiar feeling to burn in my lungs. We explored the seafloor without sharing a word. I found my goggles glittering in the fading light, but I left them where they lay. I liked it better without them anyway.

Finally, he headed back up. I followed close behind, a small smile on my face. There was the familiar ache in my lungs, but it was easier to ignore now. Holding my breath had gotten much more effortless. I began treading water as I surveyed the scene. The sun was well past noon. I nearly dropped to the bottom of the lagoon. That couldn't be true. There was no way I could stay underwater for that long without needing air.

My mind began racing. Had I inhaled some of him during my previous near-death experience? My fear of Ripple being a god resurfaced. Did I digest part of a god? What were the consequences of that? Was that why I could hold my breath for so long? And swim so well? Why the water felt like an extension of my own body. "Did you…?" I turned to face Ripple.

He looked as surprised as I was.

"What about dry drowning? Will I have water in my lungs forever?"

He shrugged.

"And how did you do that? You don't even have shoulders!"

He would have been grinning from ear to ear if he had a mouth.

I swam towards the shore, but he saved me the trip. He gently picked me up and placed me on the rocky land, careful never to touch the ground for long. I bent down and grabbed my shirt to wipe my face and hair. "I've got to get *going*. My father usually comes home for lunch, and I'm supposed to be grounded, so…" I looked back at him, hoping he would understand. He drooped sadly in the water. "What's wrong?" I asked him, a smile playing across my lips. "Are you going to miss me too much?" I slid the shirt on and forwent socks, just jammed my feet into my shoes.

He shook his head and looked away. "I'll miss you too, Rip. And thank you. F—for everything." I slung my bag over my shoulder and turned to leave. "Wait," I said, turning back to him. He perked up immediately. "Would you want to come with me?" He brightened immediately. "No, no, that would cause a scene." He sagged again.

“Well, bye. See you tomorrow.” He came as close to me as he could without leaving the water.

“What's the matter? Can’t you leave?”

He made no move.

“That’s awful.” I looked seaward. “Are you stuck in this cove because of those rocks? What happens if it all drains?”

Ripple turned away.

“No, wait! Maybe I can help you.”

I fished in my bag until I found the skin I had used for freshwater. I poured some in my mouth and poured the rest on the ground. “Could you travel in this?”

Excitedly, he backed away and charged the shore. Thrusting out the water skin, I closed my eyes and prepared for impact. None came. I got splashed but was otherwise unharmed. I peeked into the water container to ensure he had, in fact, jumped into it. A stream jumped up to poke me in the eye. "Okay, okay, I'll respect your privacy." I corked it and slid it gently into my bag.

This was either the biggest adventure of my life or my worst mistake.

Chapter Fifteen:

Big Decisions

After stepping over the fallen log, I began recounting my steps backward.

Pause at the log.

Exit from cleft in rock.

Turn at base of mountain.

Walk through Valley of Flowers.

Turn at small pond.

Walk past gnarled tree.

Enter house from back door.

I began maneuvering through the woods, hoping I knew my way back. "Can you hear me?" I asked, eyes still fixed ahead. I turned to grab the water skin and came eye-to-eye with him. Well, if he had eyes, that is. "Oh, gods! Don't do that." I felt him jiggle as if he were laughing. It was a weird sensation. "It's nice to know you can unscrew the top. What if I get sick of you, huh? What can I do then?"

He gestured for me to keep walking. "What would happen if I bent over?" I did, just to prove my point. He stayed in the exact same position, but my notebook slid out of my bag. "Point taken." Apparently, gravity didn't work on him.

I kept walking, but he never stopped looking around. "Is this your first time out of that pool?"

He shook his head.

"Did you just get stuck there by accident?"

He shrugged.

"Not so much of an accident?"

He didn't respond.

We passed the gnarled tree and I paused. “Could you duck or something, so someone doesn’t see you?”

He sunk down into the bag a bit. The top of him still peeked out and watched me enter my house.

“Kameron!” I heard my dad roar from upstairs.

“Dad?” I said cautiously. I flipped the lip of my bag down to cover Rip.

“Where are you?”

“Down here.”

“You weren’t down there when I came through earlier!”

“Y—yes, I was,” I stuttered, terrified Rip would give himself away.

“No, you were not!”

“I just had to step outside for some fresh air. It gets stuffy up there.”

"Oh, well then…" He looked me up and down as if seeing me for the first time. "I brought lunch."

"Great, I'm starving."

We ate in relative silence. He kept glancing at me as if I were an oddity. I could feel Ripple nosing around in my bag. Every few minutes, he would brave the open, and I would feel him glide out and investigate the underside of the table. The first time I just nudged him back into the bag. As he got braver, I became more annoyed. My father began to get suspicious.

"Why are you so wet?"

"Rain," I muttered, trying to kick Rip back into my bag. Luckily my father never got the chance to think about the lack of rain.

My poorly aimed kick hit him instead of Rip, and he jumped clean out of his seat. "Thor almighty, boy! What is wrong with you?"

"Um…" I watched with wide eyes as Ripple wove out behind him. "I'm just a little stir-crazy, I guess." How he did it, I'll never know, but Ripple stretched from my bag all the way into the kitchen. Where did the extra water come from? He nosed through our baking flour; Somehow, he got some on his nose without getting the container wet. He hovered above my father's head and looked mischievously down at me.

I shook my head furiously.

"You are looking a little…" he turned around to see what I was looking at, and Ripple darted the other way. "Distracted," he finished.

"Yes, been by myself all morning just… listening to the house settle."

"Right…"

"You seem a little distracted too," I mentioned, catching him staring at me again. I turned around to see if Birger was sneaking up on me or something.

"Yes, er, have you grown?"

"Since this morning? I don't think so."

"Hmmm, you seem taller."

I shrugged and went back to eating. After a moment, he did the same. I felt anxiety welling up inside of me. Every second that ticked by added another drop to my overflowing well.

I tentatively opened my mouth to speak. "Could I go down to the workshop and—"

"No!" He cleared his throat. "No, stay here."

"What has Jaggar done today?"

"Don't start this again."

"I'm not… I just think you should talk to him. Show him who's boss."

"He didn't come in today."

It was a blatant lie, but I knew if I said anything else, we would repeat last night. Instead of facing the problem, I changed the subject. "How's Birger?"

"I sent him by a while ago."

"I haven't seen him."

He stood up quickly. "Birger?" he called.

"Dad, I'm telling you, he's not—"

"Birger!"

He ran into the kitchen, where I heard him rummaging around. Ripple popped up beside me, and I shoved him down into my bag. My father returned quickly. "Follow me. Closely, now."

I stood up and pushed Ripple inside my bag one last time. My father crept down the dirt road that led up to our house. He stopped in the middle of the road and looked around carefully.

"I don't think he just got tired and stopped in the middle of the—"

He shushed me and froze, holding up a fist and signaling for me to do the same.

"Kameron!" A hoarse whisper came floating toward us from somewhere on the right side of the road.

I felt Ripple shift in my bag at the sound of my name. I hit the side of my satchel to satisfy his curiosity. My father ran off the road and began beating away the brush.

Birger was sitting with his back against a tree trunk, looking barely conscious. Judging from the burrs and thorns dug deep into his legs, he had dragged himself there.

"Bo," my father breathed. He ran to his side and tried to help him up. Birger groaned and waved him away.

He took a stammering breath and grabbed my father's shoulder. "Jaggar," he wheezed.

My father nodded. "I—I know. Let's get you up. The house isn't that far."

Birger didn't move. "Where's Kam?" he whispered.

They both turned to look at me. "They were going to the house to look for him," Birger said, his eyes finally settling on me.

I'd half-forgotten I was there. I was frozen in the road, unable to move or speak. I barely managed to croak out, "I know."

"Kameron, they won't stop trying. What can you do?" Birger was struggling to stand and looking only at my father. His unspoken words were pleading and begging for a plan.

All my father had to say was, "I don't know."

Birger groaned. "This is where indecision brought you two. Why didn't you tell me why I was checking on him every day? I could have helped!"

"You did help; that was the problem! Look where that got you!"

"I'll recover, but *he* might not!" Birger threw a finger my way. He sighed. "I hate to bring this up again. But we both remember what happened to Linnea."

My mother. My father and I both drew in a breath, both of us obviously remembering the same day with startling clarity.

. . .

I knew something was wrong from the moment I woke up. The fog hung oppressively low, shrouding my window like a figure of death. My bare feet padded across the floor and to the door, but that was as far as I got. Voices arose from downstairs. People were yelling, and someone was stomping up the stairs. Fear gripped my young heart, and I dashed to hide under my bed. Peeking out from under the blanket that dangled over my bed, I could see a pair of familiar boots.

"Kam?" a worried voice said.

It was Birger.

"Kam!" he said again. "We have to go; wake up." He rushed forward and threw the covers off my bed. When he found I wasn't there, he dashed for the door. In his panic, he left it wide open. To this day I don't know why I hid from

Birger. I knew something was wrong, and I trusted him, yet I didn't come out.

The second set of feet came up the stairs, slowly this time. They paused halfway up and turned to speak to someone outside. "Take the woman outside. It was her treason that cursed this house. Odin may deal with her as he wishes. I'll get the boy." The voice was cold like ice and hard as steel. It was a voice that haunted my every moment.

The voice was Jaggar's.

The footsteps continued as I trembled under my bed. I saw him step into the room and survey my empty bed. I screwed my eyes shut and prayed silently that he would go away. A scream from outside my window cut off my prayer. My blood seemed to freeze. I would know that voice anywhere. That voice sang me to sleep every night and greeted me each morning. My mother was in trouble, and there was nothing I could do about it.

Jaggar turned and ran back down the stairs yelling, “Not yet! Where’s the boy?”

I climbed out from under the bed and ran to the window, hoping and praying I was wrong and that it was someone else. I threw open the shutters, expecting the fog to barricade my view but her scream seemed to have purged the air of anything but the sound of her own labored breathing.

She lay in the grass of my front yard like her floral namesake. Her white nightgown was stained red. Even from here, I could see her chest heaving for each breath. My father lay unmoving at the base of the stairs, a wound just above his ear pouring blood down his face. Birger was nowhere to be seen.

Jaggar proudly strutted from the house and surveyed the scene. He turned to some of his men guarding the edges of the woods. "Did you find the boy?"

They shook their heads.

"No matter," Jaggar raised his voice. "Let this show what happens when someone defies me—defies the gods!"

Jaggar turned back to one of his men. The wind lifted his words to my ears. "Make it so that we were never here." The man nodded and ran to hide any evidence of their arrival. Jaggar turned, and his eyes swept the house. I ducked, but before I had hidden, his eyes met mine, and he grinned.

. . .

They had killed my mother. Why? That I may never know. I was beginning to wonder if it wasn't a political statement like my death would be. Or maybe the past really did repeat itself. Jaggar was trying to erase the old gods now; maybe his plan had never changed. My mother had that book of old gods and knew Balter's Ballad by heart. Could they have killed her for that?

The severity of the situation was beginning to drown me. Birger was badly hurt, my father was somewhere between a rock and a hard place, and I…

I was a dead man walking.

I squeezed my eyes shut, trying to hear past the pounding of my heart in my ears. All I could see when I closed my eyes was how differently this could have gone. What if Birger hadn't survived this attack? What would that do to me, to my father, to the whole village?

I felt Ripple nosing around me, trying to get me to explain what was going on. I didn't respond, but I didn't push him back into the bag either. I just let him be.

I also imagined what might have happened if my father hadn't been around to help Birger. There was no way I would be any help to Birger now. Especially not with a target on my back.

"I love him too, you know," said Birger. I jumped a little as my eyes flew open. Had they been having a conversation this whole time? They didn't know everything that was running through my head. "And after today, I know just how far Jaggar will go to get what he wants."

"Why not just kill me then?" my father yelled into the trees as if Jaggar's men were still listening.

They kept bickering, but I was staring intently at my shoes. "Fear," I whispered. Ripple peeked out to look at me.

He gave me a determined look, and I looked up aggressively. My mind was made up. Louder, I said, "If he keeps you afraid, he keeps you under his thumb. As long as I'm around, that'll keep happening."

They turned to look at me. Birger saw the determination in my eyes. "No, no, no," he pleaded. "Don't do anything rash."

I shuffled backward. Birger couldn't walk, let alone run, and my father held him up. By the time they'd worked it out for my father to go after me, I would have a several-minute head start. Better yet, I knew my destination, they did not.

"Hang on to hope," I whispered to both of them. Then I turned on a dime and ran up the road back toward the house.

Chapter Sixteen:

Horizons of Hope

"Kam!" they shouted in unison.

My father yelled, "Come back!" several times before trying a different tactic. "We'll figure something out!" he roared after me.

I grit my teeth and kept running. *Just don't turn around*, I commanded myself. My bag bounced on my thigh, and Ripple splashed around beside me excitedly. I didn't even stop at the house, but blew straight past it and into the woods.

My father was after me now. I could hear him thundering behind me, trampling bushes and scattering rocks under his feet. If I were running in a straight line, he might have caught up with me. But I knew the path well, and he thought I had gone inside the house. That bought me a couple more minutes.

The back door had been completely abandoned.

I barely noticed the gnarled tree.

I darted right at the small pond.

My heart hurt as I watched dozens of linneas get trampled under my feet as I ran through the valley of flowers.

At the base of the mountain, I veered right.

I only stopped when I found the cleft in the rock.

After taking a deep breath, I ducked under the log.

There hadn't been any sounds behind me for most of the journey, but that didn't mean he wasn't looking. By now, he probably had the entire town searching for me. I plopped down on the sand and kicked off my shoes. The soft waves touched the tips of my toes as I tried to catch my breath.

Ripple glided out to look at me.

"What was I thinking?" I asked him. "Running away? On an island! I'd have to be the dumbest person to ever live."

He cocked his head again.

"It would be better off for everyone if I left. Especially my father. The island would probably be rid of Jaggar in a day after that."

Ripple perked up. He pointed to the water.

"I don't feel like a swim right now, sorry Rip." It was a lie, of course. Every part of me was itching to get wet again.

He pointed even more, but I ignored him and kept sulking. He reached up and slapped me.

"Hey!" I rubbed my face that was now wet and red. "What was that for?"

He pointed to the water.

"Knock yourself out!" I threw the canister he was riding in towards the middle of the pool. He splashed harmlessly into the water and didn't resurface. "I'll need that water skin back!" I yelled over the water. It shot out of the water and hit me square in the nose.

"What is wrong with you? I'm the one who just destroyed my reputation and the relationship with my father! Why are *you* mad?"

He popped out of the water and made a dramatic effort to point down.

"I have a random question," I said, just to annoy him. He made an effort to sag and look frustrated. "Since I accidentally ingested some of you… does that come with any long-term consequences? Could you just appear in my bath one day?" The look he gave me made it clear that I'd given him an idea. "I will hurl you out a window faster than you can say *naked*."

He pointed one last time.

"No, you're being rude. I don't appreciate it." I knew I was being selfish and harsh. I also knew I was losing an argument to a pillar of water. That one hit my self-esteem hard.

My feet were still in the surf, and before long, the water began creeping up my legs. "Stop it." I pushed at it. Surprisingly enough, it worked the first couple of times. Then he got tired of dealing with me and just jerked me into the water. I opened my mouth to curse him, but it ended up garbled and unintelligible. I saw a vague outline of him guiding me toward the center of the pool.

He pointed downward as if saying, "Why not just stay here?"

I tried to say "I can't hide forever! We need a better plan." But it came out as more of a jumbled mess. Nevertheless, he seemed to understand what I meant.

Directly behind me, a giant rock crashed into the water with so much force I flinched. It sank in a flurry of bubbles, and I glared at Rip. "What was that for?" I shouted.

He shrugged. "Wasn't me," he conveyed.

I looked up to see another rock plummeting our way. Rip hurled me out of the way, and I sailed onto the shore so hard the breath was knocked from my lungs. He bent over me, worry plain in his face of foggy water.

Another rock tumbled into the cove's opening, and my gaze followed it down into the water, further blocking where the lagoon connected to the ocean. My eyes snapped up to the top of the ridge. A figure stood on the edge of the cliff overhead, using a long staff to topple the rocks into the water. I frantically pushed Rip back into the canteen. “Who is it?” I whispered. Rip shook his head and slowly retreated back into the container.

I dove into the water and Rip lifted us towards the person. I stepped onto the sparse grass of the cliff edge and Rip gathered himself back into the water skin. I stalked behind a tree to watch someone haul over more rocks to lug over the edge. As they turned, I launched into action.

Filled with renewed courage and energy, I tackled them to the ground.

“Kovah?”

His blond hair had fallen across his face, but there was no mistaking his identity. “Rowan?” I thought I would be the terrified one, but he looked like he’d seen a ghost.

“You’re dead!”

Chapter Seventeen:

Caught

"What are you doing here?" I demanded.

He stared up at me as if he were seeing me for the first time. He shook off his daze and his expression hardened. "I could ask you the same thing."

"Why should I be dead?"

As if realizing his mistake, he clamped his mouth shut.

"What are you doing up here?"

He averted his eyes.

"You better start talking, or I'll—"

"What are you going to do, little Kovah? Call daddy?"

Anger swelled inside of me. I stood up and he grinned. I surprised myself with my strength as I lugged him to the cliffside. With one hand, I held the scruff of his shirt, with the other I dropped my water skin over the edge and into the ocean. Rowan's eyes followed it all the way down until it splashed into the waves. His gaze slowly drifted back to me, where his eyebrows knit together in confusion. He glanced down at my feet, then back at my face. Our eyes were finally even. Now with both hands free, I propped him up on the edge. "Start talking."

He spit in my face. "Make me."

I raised my eyebrows in response, a small grin tugged at the corner of my mouth. How long had I waited for this moment? This was payback for years of torment and a lifetime of living destitute. One by one, I pried my fingers off. I was able to see an instant of surprise on his face before he dropped out of sight. A dishonorable scream sprung from his lungs. Rip brought him back to me again. When he was dumped at my feet, he was dripping brine and pale as a sheet. I leaned forward and put my hands on his shoulders. "I'll ask you again," I said quietly, "What are you doing up here?"

"My father told me to pile rocks on the cove entrance every day."

"Why?"

"I don't know."

I leaned him back a little more.

"I don't know, honest! He told me never to look down and to never go into the cove."

"You never did?"

He paused. "A creature lives down there," he said finally. "A terrible, evil, vile—"

I felt a familiar cool touch on my cheek as Rip popped up from behind my shoulder. Rowan screamed again as I smiled and Rip handed me my canteen.

"You're a traitor!" He shrieked. "Do you know what that is?"

I turned to look at him. Rip met my gaze. "Not really," I admitted. "But he's treated me with more kindness than any of my own people ever did." I turned and thrust him onto the ground. "Why should I be dead?"

"My father sent men to your house, said you'd been fraternizing with the enemy," he eyed Rip carefully.

"Where is my father?"

"As soon as my father put out the call for The Horde to find you, he said you'd disappeared. I thought he'd just told you to run. The whole island is looking for you now."

I walked away slowly. Rip rested on my left shoulder, now sitting comfy in the water skin tied to my belt. "What should we do?" I whispered.

Rip nodded to the cliff edge.

"No, no, I can't do that twice!" Rowan said, trying to scramble away.

Rip stretched out and tripped Rowan and dragged him to the cliff edge again.

Rip pointed down at the ocean.

"Hiding isn't a plan!" Rip looked away, back towards the island. My mind began to swirl. *Maybe I could strike a deal with him?* I wondered. I doubted its success, but it was worth a try. I took a deep breath and turned around.

He was gone.

I scanned the trees, but everything was quiet. Rowan had seen his chance and taken it. Half the village would be on its way up here if I didn't move now.

"Well, we're dead. We are very, very dead." Rip disappeared into the canteen. "You can't hide from this!" I said into the mouth of the bottle. "You're in just as much trouble as I am."

A little stream of water came out of the top and snapped the lid shut. I shook my head and took a step toward the edge of the cliff. "How long can we hold our breath? Would swimming away be an option?"

Rip's head appeared, and he nodded.

"We'd need supplies for a long trip."

He nodded again.

"How do you feel about petty thievery?"

He shrugged.

A smile crept across my face. “How much more trouble can we get into, right?” I ran through the woods, dodging low-hanging branches and curled roots as I went.

Something throttled me from behind, and I pitched forward and crashed into a tree. I seemed to be moving in slow motion. My head throbbed, and it hurt to move at all. I rolled over and fiddled with my belt loop. I cracked open my eyes only to see that the canteen had rolled hopelessly out of reach.

Rowan stood over me, knife in hand. “I’m going to take you to my father, Kovah.”

I sat up slowly, hoping the ringing in my ears would quiet down. He bent down and held the knife to my throat. “Don’t make another sound, or you’ll never make it back to Eztenburg at all.”

I blinked hard and looked up at him. The setting sun glinted on the knife. His eyes were wild with emotion. His hair was crazy, still wet from his swim earlier.

"Do it," I croaked. "I won't stop you." I laid back down, fighting down the bile in my throat. My statement surprised both of us. Ever since I'd met Rip, my brave stupidity had increased tenfold. It was easy to say that now was my peak for blind bravery.

He looked confused but took a step forward.

"Go on," I urged. "Our tussle on the cliff earlier proves I can't bluff." I should have been terrified, but I wasn't. Now that my life was actually being threatened, my mind was clear, and I was calmer than ever.

The obvious befuddlement on his face was almost comical. "Why?"

"I always expected to die at the hands of a Jaggar. I just didn't think it would be you."

He was quiet.

I inched up so that I was leaning back on my elbows. "Your father will kill me, you realize that right?" He didn't say a word. "But he will not permit me the honor of a swift and private death. He will draw it out in front of crowds. Make an example of me. I would much rather you get it over with now."

"Do you know no fear? I have the weapon of your destruction in my hands right now!"

I looked from his face to the knife in his trembling hands. It was lowered a bit. "I have experienced more fear than I should. Petty fears of things that could never hurt me, and grave fears of things that could kill me. I know plenty of fear, but not of you."

"Why not?"

I couldn't fight the slight smile creeping across my face. "Because if you were going to kill me, then you would have done it already."

Rip grabbed the knife from his hands and pushed him down beside me. I jumped up and stood above him.

"Why did you have a knife?" I asked as I re-tied Rip to my belt loop.

"Why do you have a monster?" Rowan spat from the ground.

"He's not a monster."

"Then what is that thing?"

"I—I don't know."

He slowly stood up. Rip rose to my shoulder height. He looked at Rip then back at me.

"Look, Rowan, I have to get off this island."

"Why?"

"Because your father *really* is going to kill me. That part wasn't a joke. Now stop getting in my way and let me leave!"

"I can't!"

"Yes, you can! Just take two steps to the right and let me through!"

"You'll tell everyone I let you go, and then he'll blame me."

"No, I won't."

"Why wouldn't you? You have every reason to!"

"Because," I took a deep breath and finally unclenched my hands, "I know how it feels to live in the shadow of your father."

His face darkened and he turned away.

"You didn't tell anyone you saw me, right?"

"No, but I'm about to."

"Then why didn't you already?"

He didn't answer.

"Look, I know this is going to sound completely crazy."

"It already does."

"Then this is going to sound insane, but hear me out. Okay?"

He nodded, eyeing my belt where Ripple was beginning to snake out again. I tried to redirect his attention. "You and I both know that Jaggar runs Eztenburg. He's already corrupted the counsel. He's trying to get my dad to play into his hands, so he's threatened to kill me."

"He killed your mom."

I took a step back.

"How did you know that?"

Rowan sat down on a nearby stump. “Your dad was going to press for our borders to open, and my dad didn’t like the idea. So… he threatened your mother.”

I sat heavily on the ground in front of him.

“He fought back, your dad. So, my dad found ‘dirt’ on your mother, things he knew people would question. When your dad didn’t give in he…” Rowan shook his head. “My father came home that day more excited than I’d ever seen him.”

I closed my eyes as the scene unfolded in front of me. My mother was never one to take heckling from anyone, even my father. They would argue until they were blue in the face if they had the chance. I squeezed my eyes shut against the array of images bombarding me.

“How do you know all of this?” I whispered

"Overheard him telling another counsel member about it."

I dropped my head into my hands. Rip glided out and rested his head on my knee.

"Kam?" I looked up. Rowan's eyes were red-rimmed as they met mine. "I want to help you, really, I do." He sighed. "But I know my dad. Your father *has* to give in if he wants to keep you alive."

"I know, I know, " I said, "but he doesn't want me to be killed. What's stopping Jaggar from doing this again? Birger was already attacked once, and I'm next. The only way to keep Eztenburg out of Jaggar's hands is for my dad to stand against him. For that to happen, I can't be at risk."

"So you're leaving? Just like that?"

"Yes."

“With that?” He pointed to Ripple, who had crept further out of the water skin and was now eyeing him carefully.

“Yes.”

I saw the gears turning in his head. “It won’t work,” he said.

“What do you mean?” I was offended now. “It has to work.” It was my only plan.

“As long as your dad thinks you’re alive, he’ll keep searching for you.”

“What are you suggesting?” I feared what his answer would be.

“I think the only way to really get your dad to do something… is if you *were* dead.”

Chapter Eighteen:

Against All Reason

I can't believe I'm doing this. How in the name of Odin did he convince me of this? *I could still turn back now,* I thought, wishing I could convince myself. Maybe Rip was right; maybe I could hide out until everyone forgot about me.

But one glance at Rowan's fading figure brought back the memory of that moment. He had been right; the realization of it washed over me like a tidal wave. Birger would never stop looking for me if I disappeared. The town would stay under Jaggar's thumb forever if I simply ran the other way. They needed a catalyst—a martyr.

I watched him turn and head back into the trees after we'd made our plan. Could I really trust him after so many years of ill will between us? Do people really change? He turned and looked back at me before disappearing into the foliage. Our eyes met, and I knew I had no choice. He was my only hope if I wanted this plan to work, if I wanted to live.

I looked down at Rip, gazing intently at the spot where Rowan had disappeared. He swirled anxiously like he was also scared. "What do you think, Rip? Is this the right thing to do?"

He looked up at me, then surveyed the island from our perch on the cliffside. I knew we were both straining our ears, waiting for the shouts and echoing footfalls of the approaching mob. They would come, and I would be powerless to stop them.

I stepped to the edge of the cliff and took a deep breath before letting myself fall. I knew Rip would catch me, but my heart still jumped into my throat. We splashed harmlessly into the water that rose to meet me before Rip set me back down gently in the knee-deep water.

I made it to the cove and picked up my satchel only to occupy my mind. So many thoughts raged behind my eyes. I carefully unclipped the waterskin from my belt and set it in the water. Ripple rose up to meet me. He watched me fiddle with gadgets I would never get to finish. I could sense his heightened sadness as he swept forward to put a hand on my knee.

I paused my tinkering but didn't look at him. "Maybe we should go ahead and do this," I said aloud. "He's bringing them soon."

Rip didn't move, but I took off my satchel and threw it on the shore. I trekked into the water, loving the feeling it gave me. I wanted to swim these familiar waters one last time, but I knew the clock was ticking. Unlike earlier, the water didn't swish off of me. It seemed to cling to me. It begged me to reconsider the plan. I swam towards the rocks at the mouth of the cove. "This is going to work, right?"

Ripple offered no condolences. I kept my head down and swam faster. We reached the rocks, and I had to tread water for an instant. A pillar of water lifted me from the cove and over the rocky barricade Rowan had built. Rip sat me where I could look over the ocean but easily climb down. The sea outside the cove looked angry. The waves ran headlong into the cliffside with giant clouds of mist swirling up toward me. Below us, the waves beat against the rocks, but no water came into the cove. Jaggar's plan would have worked if not for me. He might have cut Rip off from the ocean and eventually killed him. Who knows how long Rowan had been adding rocks to this wall, but I was about to undo all that work.

I held the waterskin aloft, and Rip jumped in. Without Rip to guide it, all the other water in the cove fell away. “Ready?” I said, gripping the waterskin a little tighter.

He nodded and seemed to settle himself tighter into the canteen.

I reared back and threw the flask with all the strength I could muster. He sailed out a good distance into the open ocean before plummeting into the turbulent waters below. I waited, my heart pounding, hoping I hadn’t hurt him. Just when I was beginning to consider jumping in after him, a blob of water rose from the waves and nodded at me.

This was it. Now I was really alone, no one left to guide me. I couldn’t hide behind Birger or Rip now, any hope I had of surviving tonight rested with me. I pushed my back against the cold jagged edge of the cliffside and put up my hand to shade my eyes from the setting sun.

My last look at the cove. It was just as beautiful as the day I'd stumbled into it accidentally. A million moments flashed through my mind like lightning.

The first time he had saved my life.

Then the second, a little bit later.

Every laugh, every adventure, every second he had kept me lashed to this life flashed through my eyes in an instant. All those memories seemed a little bittersweet. They were tinted with a passing time and victim of my circumstance. I would never dance under those crystal waters with him or roam the woods with him at my side. All those days were gone, and they were never coming back.

The climb down from the dam was much more perilous than getting up. Rip wasn't down there to catch me now, only sharp rocks. Once I was close enough to the water to see where the large stones had fallen, I pushed off and dove into the water. When I surfaced, the sky was dark, and the stars were beginning to peek out. There wasn't a cloud in the sky. Instead of thinking about the next part of the plan like I probably should have been, I began backstroking so I could stare at the stars for a little longer.

I smiled as a familiar constellation came into view. The Gateway to the Gods. Another memory of my mother shouted over the clamor of other voices in my mind. We had been stargazing only a few days before Jaggar came for her in our front yard. When she'd pointed it out, I asked why it had such an odd name.

"Because that's the door that men's souls go through after they die," she'd answered.

If she was right, I might find myself crossing that threshold much sooner than I'd expected.

My hands brushed the shore, and I stood up, shaking the water from my hair. I splashed up and sat on the shore to dry off before the mob came to fetch me. The sand was still warm underneath me, and the soft waves curled around my toes. When would I have this kind of quiet again? I stretched out on my back with one arm resting on my stomach, counting each rise and fall, and the other arm was bent under my head serving as a makeshift pillow.

I wondered vaguely if the gods had ordained this. Had they seen this outcome when Rip and I first met? Had they laughed at my misfortune as my father locked me away? Had they called in their families to watch as I failed miserably to escape?

Or perhaps I had been judging them too harshly.

Were they watching with white knuckles and red eyes? Had they stopped their daily lives to hope against all reason that I succeeded? Were they on my side? Were they cursing Jaggar? Were they pulling for our plan?

Maybe I was overthinking all of this.

I closed my eyes and hoped for the best.

The one thing I didn't account for was my own exhaustion. Although I don't know how, I must have fallen asleep. My eyes fluttered open to the sounds of shouts and alarms. I sat bolt upright and found only darkness. Branches snapped behind me, and I whirled around. Pinpricks of light were dancing through the trees, heading my way.

It was showtime.

Although Jaggar had never fought in any wars, he used war tactics now. He had his men stretch out in a wide crescent, cutting off any chance of escape. I slung my bag over my shoulder and scrambled to my feet. My heart pounded and I desperately wished for Rip to be by my side. My bare feet dashed across the sand and into the tree line.

Just one more second, I prayed. *One more moment alone before the crazy.*

If the gods were listening, they didn't answer my prayer. I peeked out from behind the tree, hoping to see anyone before they saw me. Sadly, I was too slow. Something sharp touched my back and I froze.

"I've found him." The statement should have been for the entire crew, but he whispered it so only I could hear. I ran out from behind the tree and whirled around. It was Jaggar. I backed up, trying to keep some distance between us. I bumped into someone and tripped over a tree root. Why had I been cursed with clumsiness? I landed hard and rolled, causing pebbles to scatter. I turned to see who had caused my fall. It was my father.

"Dad?"

"Kameron?"

I scrambled backward. "Dad, I'm sorry, but I—"

Jaggar jumped forward and grabbed me.

"I've got him!" he shouted.

"Let go of my son!" My father yelled back.

"Your son is treasonous and must be treated as such," Jaggar said, jerking me as I tried to stand.

My father started forward, wanting to help me. "He's done nothing wrong!"

"*My* son does not lie." Jaggar pointed and there, amid the shadows, was Rowan. We made eye contact for a brief moment before Jaggar shook me, and I tripped again.

My father didn't answer. Rowan *did* lie. All the time, in fact. But saying that to Jaggar would only make things worse.

"What do you have to say about this, boy?" Jaggar peered down at me. "Have you broken Eztenburg's laws? Do you not regularly convene here and converse with a strange being?"

"I regularly come here," I admitted, shocking even myself with my courage. "And I do talk. Mostly to myself, though."

He reared back and slapped me. I landed hard on my backside, reeling from the shock. I put a hand to my face, eyes watering from the blow.

I saw the anger in my father's eyes as he closed the gap between him and Jaggar. "If you touch my son again—"

Jaggar turned on my father. "You'll what, Kovah?" I saw a million emotions flash across my father's face. Anger. Determination. Fear. Resignation. My father backed up as I struggled to my feet. If he was this easily subdued, my efforts may be in vain. I had to find a way to get back his fighting spirit.

"Dad," I started, "It's all true. Everything mom said, all those stories. They're true!"

Jaggar whirled around, his wild hair spinning with him into a halo around him for just an instant. "What?" he spat.

I turned to face him, shrugging off the men who tried to hold me back. "You are trying to bury the past, erase our history. But we're abandoning a part of ourselves. This has all happened before, and it'll all probably happen again!"

"You don't know what you're talking about, boy."

"I have been treated with more kindness from a creature that we as a society have turned our backs on than people I've lived among my whole life!"

Jaggar signaled to a man who grabbed me from behind.

"Just wait a minute!" my father said, rushing forward, trying to help me.

"Dad, what was it you said about people like him?" I thrust my chin out at Jaggar since the man behind me held my arms fast.

I watched my father's gears turn as he tried to remember which instance I was talking about. I saw the change come over him as his words came back to him. "History will prove," he began, "that every time a villainous man comes to power, he finds his dominion all too small."

Jaggar ground his teeth angrily. "Your son can't be trusted. He's admitted to treason. Every word he says is a lie!"

My bravery was growing. It swelled in my chest like the sea before spitting out a storm. My heart beat wildly and I thrust my elbow backwards into the gut of my captor. I ran forward. "Listen to me—" I barely made it three steps before Jaggar thrust out his leg. I tumbled to the ground, rocks cutting my hands and face. Just as I rolled over to curse Jaggar's name, I saw him bringing the blunt end of his sword down on me.

Chapter Nineteen:

Deathbed Confessions

My temples ached. It hurt to open my eyes and to move my jaw. The floor I was laying on was surprisingly cold. I cracked open an eye to see thick iron bars in front of me. Those wouldn't have moved even if I had the strength to try. How long have I been here? Every second I was cooped up was like a needle in my skin. Only when your minutes are numbered do you begin to carefully craft how you want to spend them. I was all too aware that each breath brought me closer to my last.

My hairline felt sticky when I raised my hand to tenderly probe the area. In the soft moonlight streaming through the window behind me, I could see that my fingers were tainted with blood. Someone shuffled nearby and I jumped.

"Kam?" a voice said.

I sat up slowly, trying in vain to wipe the blood from my scalp. "Dad?"

He stepped closer to the bars and the line of moonlight fell across his weary face. "H—How are you?" he asked, wringing the hem of his shirt nervously.

"Good, given the circumstances." I smiled, but he didn't share my humor.

"Birger would have stopped by, but…" He didn't continue.

"Just—" I stopped, my breath seemingly stuck in my throat. "Just tell him I said goodbye."

He nodded and wiped his eyes, trying to hide his tears.

"Dad," I took a deep breath. "I am so, so sorry." I stood up slowly and stumbled against the wall for support. My legs were numb and tingly from sitting in my odd position so long. He reached through the bars, trying to help me, but I was still out of his reach. I saw the anger in his eyes when he came up short. He grabbed the bars and shook them with a roar that would have felled even Thor.

I stepped forward and put my head against the bars. "Dad, it's okay. I'm okay."

"*I* am the one who should be sorry." He put his head against mine. "Maybe if I had just listened to you, this wouldn't have happened. I shouldn't have let history repeat itself."

The whole ordeal may have been avoidable if he had been this approachable before now, but I couldn't say that to him.

“Can you do something for me?” I asked quietly.

Not bothering to lower his voice, he said, “I’ll break you out.”

“No,” I smiled, “that's not what I was thinking about.”

“Just say the word. I can pull some favors. I’ll—”

“Thanks, dad, but no. Where would I go anyway?” He dropped his eyes. “Can you promise not to mourn too long before—” a strangled sob escaped him, cutting me short. Giant tears streamed into his beard. It took me a moment to find the strength to continue. “Before you get Jaggar back?”

More tears trickled down his face as he tried to find words. He came up short and clasped my hands tightly with a nod. We sat there, holding each other through the bars, heads pressed together, until Jaggar came to run him out.

After that, I sat alone with my head resting on my knees. Jaggar paced in front of my cell every few minutes, just to ensure I hadn't escaped. I didn't intend to— not yet, at least. Every time I heard him come by, I turned away. He didn't deserve the satisfaction of seeing the fear in my eyes. When he wasn't nearby, I lifted my head to the moonlight.

Where was Rip right now? Was he as nervous as I was? Were we both staring up at the moon, counting the minutes until my demise?

"Kam?"

I jumped and whirled around. I hadn't heard anyone come in, but Birger stood by the bars of my cell, real as the walls but quiet as a phantom.

"Jaggar said I'm not allowed back here," he let out a breathy laugh that sounded like a whale blowing out air through its blow hole. “As if he could stop me. Look, I wanted to bring you this.”

He handed me a small pouch that jingled when it fell into my hands.

“Money?” I asked, confused.

Birger nodded and threw a glance behind him. “Jaggar’s bribe money. Never spent a cent he gave me. Figured you would find a better use for it.”

I raised an eyebrow.

“Come on, boy, I know you. Drop the act. I know you have a plan. Tell me, how are you getting out of this one?”

Wicked smiles spread over both our faces as I slid the money pouch into one of my many pockets. It rattled at my side in the nearly empty area. Jaggar had confiscated anything I might use as a weapon or pick the lock. Pity. I would have loved to chuck a hammer at his head as my final act.

A door clanged, and we both whirled around. Jaggar murmured something, and Birger turned back to me. I reached out and put a hand on the bar. He wrapped his strong, calloused hands around my slender fingers. "I'll see you in a little bit."

A muffled reply answered Jaggar as Birger slipped quietly away. More yelling came soon after that, but I never heard Birger's voice. He must have gotten away.

"Let me see him!"

"He's going to be executed in a few hours. Why do you care?"

"I don't! Just— just let me gloat a second, dad. *I* told you where he was! *I* turned him in!"

There was a moment of silence as Jaggar weighed the risks. "Fine. You get ten minutes."

Rowan appeared from the darkness. His hair was pulled back again. He looked fresher than I did, but in his eyes, I saw the same thing I'd been feeling all night. He knelt down in front of me and put his hand on the bars.

"Kameron?" he said.

I shuffled forward so we could whisper. "Call me Kam," I said with a shrug. The hint of a smile tugged at his mouth, but it was hard to smile when the musk of the jail filled your nose, and the dimness of my situation was in his face.

"Are you okay?"

"Never better," I said dryly.

I saw Jaggar watching us out of the corner of my eye. I sat beside him and gave a small gesture to let him know his dad was watching.

"Do you have a preference?"

A shiver ran down my spine, but it wasn't from the damp air surrounding us. "On how I die?" The words felt strange on my lips. I never thought I would find myself answering that question.

He bowed his head, but his eyes never left mine.

"Not exactly."

"Do you have a way you *don't* want them to… do it? Maybe I can speak on your behalf."

I met his eyes finally. "Don't tell anyone," I said. A quick glance behind Rowan confirmed that Jaggar was listening. He leaned in expectantly, waiting for me to spill my secrets. "I'm terrified of heights. The cliff on the East side of the island has always terrified me. Whatever happens, don't let make me go near there."

Rowan nodded, but my eyes were on the dim outline of Jaggar. As he turned to go, I saw the smile on his face. He'd taken the bait.

"They'll come for you at dawn," Rowan said. His shoulders were tense until we heard Jaggar's footsteps finally fade away. I could barely comprehend what he'd said. *Dawn.* The night had never seemed so short.

Once I was sure he was gone, I whispered, "Rowan?"

He looked up again. He met my eyes and saw all the fear I couldn't hide.

"I'm about to die." The reality of our situation had finally settled on us and seemed to press the air from my chest. I desperately wished Ripple were here with me. I missed his comforting presence like I would miss my right arm. "How sure are you that this is going to work?"

He looked away. "Certain."

A deep silence followed. Instead of dwelling on the pressing fear, I looked past it and towards the hopefully future. If I made it that far, that is. “What am I supposed to do afterward?”

“Whatever you want. You can be free.”

I smiled feebly. “I don’t suppose this would even begin to cover it, but thank you. For everything.”

He nodded slowly.

“What made you decide to help me?”

He finally looked up. His voice was low, but I barely managed to catch his words. “No one stands up to my father, not even me. I see the fear in people as he walks by. Until recently, I never knew the atrocities he’d committed. Do you remember that day at the old temple?”

“That was you?”

He nodded. "You disappeared, but I followed your footprints into the main area and read what you'd found."

"Bury the forsaken," I breathed.

"I did some digging after that. I actually began to think before following orders. One night when I was dumping rocks, you just climbed up over the edge. I—I'm sorry. I didn't mean to hurt you, you just scared me. I thought you were my father. He doesn't like anything but blind obedience."

"It was you?"

He nodded. "I'm sorry, I don't know what I was thinking."

"That's when I met Rip. He saved me that night."

A slight smile spread over his face. "Maybe all things do work together for good, even when you intend them for evil. After that night, I realized how much like him I had become. I decided I didn't want to be a part of all the hurt he had caused. I'm sorry I didn't speak up sooner."

This time it was me who smiled. "Better late than never."

Chapter Twenty:

The Death of Kameron Kovah

The light crawling into my cell pulled me into the day I dreaded.

Jaggar dragged Rowan away an hour or two before the sky started showing the first signs of light. I quietly promised him that he would see me again, despite the longevity of my absence. I couldn't sleep. I couldn't think outside the small circles my mind wove in.

Could this be the end of Jaggar's long and terrible reign?

I'm going to die.

Jaggar.

My execution.

Just before dawn, Jaggar came and unlocked my cell. I pushed my back against the far wall, but he jerked me up and pulled me out the door.

"Where are we going?"My voice trembled, and my body shook involuntarily. Instead of answering, he just smiled. That's when I knew exactly where we were going: the cliff.

On the way to the door, he grabbed a length of rope and tied my hands behind my back. When I protested, he seized a potato sack and pulled it over my head.

Now he was just being cruel. No one in the history of Eztenburg had been blinded as they died. It was an injustice. It took away any hope of begging the gods for entrance into Valhalla, the afterlife for warriors and heroes who died in battle. This was the final shred of dignity he could take from me.

On our parade through the square and to the cliffs, Jaggar kept a tight hold on the rope binding my hands. He did nothing to stop me from tripping and falling over every branch and loose stone we came across. I had no way to catch myself, so my knees were cut and bleeding before we'd even made it out of town. Although he had no issue with watching me fall, he barked orders and insults at me as I got up.

I hated this blindness. The sack stuck to my mouth, and my breathing became labored. I was going to suffocate under this.

The walk to the cliff gave me plenty of time to be sad. Jaggar growled threats at me, but it became easier and easier to ignore him. There were so many things I would miss.

The cove and all the memories I made there.

The sunsets of fire that were drawn out by the gods.

The workshop where Birger and I had gotten to work together.

The living memory of my mother; the house I had shared with her.

The woods behind my house.

There were a thousand other things that I was thankful for, despite the bleak circumstances. That's when I realized I wasn't afraid anymore. This potato sack wasn't anything to fret about. My death seemed a much more worthy fear. I was thankful for every step, every second of quiet during that walk. All the time to think only gave me more time to dread what was coming.

The wind picked up, blowing the sack backward enough to let me smell the salty air. We'd reached the edge of the tree line. Through the rough burlap, I could see the sun rising slowly from its watery grave. It warmed my skin and took some of the jitters away. It felt close enough to touch. I stumbled again, but this time a firm hand grabbed me by the arm. As Jaggar paraded me forward, a collective intake of breath traveled around me. There must have been a large group of onlookers. Murmurs grew loud enough to cover the sound of rushing water.

Jaggar led me forward still. With each step, the sound of the waves crashing into the bottom of the cliffs grew. Rocks scattered under my feet, and the grass that had been grabbing at my boots rapidly disappeared. I bucked up and refused to move any farther; the cliff edge couldn't be far from me now.

Turning from my doom, I put my face towards my people. I refused to go down in our record book as the boy who shrank back in fear of his own people.

"Citizens of Eztenburg!" Jaggar announced dramatically. "I give you the traitor who threatens our shores!" He thumped me hard on the back. I lost my footing, and a gasp rippled through the crowd. I righted myself and stood tall. "He is sentenced to death! So let the very waves he wished to be his savior be his end." He gripped my arm tightly.

He was about to push me when I shouted, "Wait!" he paused long enough to let me shake the potato sack from my head. The crowd gasped again as if they had forgotten what I looked like.

That wasn't promising.

"I have a few words before I go," I said, blowing my hair from my eyes.

Jaggar nodded angrily but never let go of my arm.

"I, Kameron Kovah the Fourth, son of Kameron Kabble Kovah the Third, has been wrongly tried and judged. Jaggar publicly demands that we evolve and forget our past, but he schemes for our downfall. He privately executes any who stands in his way. Look around you. How many people could still be breathing here with you if we had realized Jaggar's plans sooner? He has built his throne out of blood and lies. How many more will die before we realize that he is the one causing the disunity? What happens today is because his iron fist is squeezing all of Eztenburg. Surely, you feel it as I do. We eradicated our chief long ago because of the fear of corrupting powers. Jaggar would have all of Eztenburg in his clutches, but my father was all that stood between him and complete control."

My gaze flickered toward my dad. He stood next to Birger, who had a hand on his shoulder. They both looked as shaken as I felt.

"When my father stood against him, Jaggar stooped to bribery. When my father was unfazed, the threats came soon afterward. He killed my mother, Linnea Kovah, and now he has come for me. I was all that stood between Jaggar and my father's support. Once I am gone, I trust that you will do what should have been done long before now." I turned to look Jaggar in the eye. His greasy hair was whipped wildly in the same wind that ruffled mine. The grip on my arm tightened. The look in his eyes told me that throwing me over the cliff prematurely wasn't out of the cards yet.

I took a deep breath before continuing. "I—"

"Wait!" A murmur ran through the crowd as they tried to find who'd spoken. Rowan pushed his way to the front. "Wait!" he cried again as he ran forward.

"I have worked with Kam for years. I know my father better than anyone. His business is one of shadows and deceit. Kam has done nothing wrong!"

He turned to face me and his father. The hatred in Jaggar's eyes would have burned a hole through anyone else, but Rowan stood tall. Rowan's stormy gaze finally fell on me as he tucked my notebook into a pocket of my nearly empty apron.

"You left this behind," he whispered.

"Get out of the way!" Jaggar hissed.

The wind blew Rowan's hair back, and for an instant, he looked like a warrior ready for battle. Jaggar flinched, but Rowan didn't so much as blink. Rowan turned back to me and I noticed that he had tears in his eyes. "That last page looks interesting."

My eyebrows furrowed. I hadn't written anything on the last page.

He looked back up at his father. "I'm not going to let history repeat itself. It's time the Jaggar name turned a new leaf." Rowan turned and marched back to the band of people watching intently.

Jaggar fumbled for words. "Is that all?" He said impatiently.

I rolled my shoulders, trying to loosen his hold on my arm. It worked. I felt his grip slip just a little. "Don't rush me. This is my death, not yours. Well, not yet, anyway." I didn't actually have anything else to say, but I wasn't in any hurry to die.

People were beginning to shout and come forward. My father was chief among them. His eyes wielded the full fury of Odin. I wouldn't have been surprised if he struck Jaggar down right there. Birger was right behind him, wiping the sweat from his bald head and preparing for a fight. "Dad—" I started but never got to finish. With an impatient roll of his eyes, Jaggar's grip returned to my arm. He slung me backward with all his strength, and I flew off the side of the cliff. I heard the heartbreaking sound of Birger and my Father calling my name one last time.

My body felt the free fall before my mind registered what had happened. Rowan had slipped me a knife only moments before, so I had been working at the rope. When my hands were finally free, I rotated in the air so I could see the ocean roaring up to meet me.

I didn't have time to whisper a prayer. All I could do was close my eyes and brace for impact.

Epilogue

I expected the sharp slap of my body hitting the water like a wall, but instead, it was like falling into a warm bed after a long day in the cold. The waves cradled me like a newborn, and I sank softly into them. Once I was sure I wasn't dead, I swam deeper. Lower and lower I sank, until the darkness around me lengthened into inky midnight. I opened my eyes to only see bubbles around me. Something brushed my leg, and I looked down.

Only darkness greeted me.

A warm stream brushed my face, and I smiled. It was Rip. He swished around me, making sure I wasn't hurt. I could have kissed him I was so happy. We waited in the darkness for a few more minutes, hoping everything went according to plan. When nothing immediately happened, we both got fidgety. My heart beat loudly in my ears, and Rip swished restlessly around my shoulders. We swam upwards to get a better view. Not close enough for anyone up top to see me, but close enough to see the sunlight dancing on the surface of the water. Ripple and I hovered, hoping against hope for a miracle.

Just when I was beginning to think I had faked my death for nothing, something big slapped the water. I gestured to Ripple, and he shot up and grabbed whatever had fallen. He pulled it down to be level with me.

It was Jaggar.

His eyes widened when he recognized me. I flashed a wicked grin at him as the fear in his eyes grew. He thrashed around and fought against the water that held him, but only one of us would survive this trip. I nodded to Ripple, and Jaggar was dragged down, a gush of bubbles streaming from his mouth in a silent scream.

I waited, even after Ripple had rejoined me. Nothing happened for a long time. A relieved smile spread across my face.

It worked.

I hadn't hit the rocks. Ripple hadn't failed me. Rowan had riled up the crowd into a mob. My father had finally gotten rid of Jaggar. Eztenburg was free.

And so was I.

Ripple and I began swimming away, hoping to find land. We headed toward the sun in the East. Swishing as easily as dolphins as we glided through the sun-kissed waters.

After a few hours, the ocean floor steadily rose to meet us. The swells crested above us, and a dock appeared a little ways in front of us. I stood on the ocean floor and gazed up at the long supports holding the boardwalk in place. As far as I could see, no one was up there. Ripple swam into the waterskin as I reattached it to my belt, and I swam upward. My head breached the water, and I grabbed the edge of the dock in the same swift moment. My original calculation had been slightly off. Several fishermen sat on the edges of the dock, cleaning their gear. Their eyes grew wide as I climbed out of the water and shook the water from my hair. I didn't meet their eyes as I strode over the dock and into town.

The meager supplies I brought wouldn't go far. I had a handful of Eztenburg coins, my notebook, my nearly empty tool belt, an apron, and Rip, of course. When I bought a sandwich from a small shop around the corner, the lady seemed surprised when I handed her the gold coins, but she didn't ask where they came from.

With Rip at my side, a warm sandwich in my hand, and a brand new world to explore, I couldn't wipe the smile from my face. I had never done anything by myself. It was nerve-wracking. Everyone watched me curiously as I scurried about, trying to memorize everything I saw. I never knew people could look so diverse. This city was full of buildings that stretched way over my head. The only mountain was way in the distance. Colors and smells I didn't even know existed assaulted me.

After a while of exploring, I found a quiet alleyway and sat down. Not even the screaming of my tired feet could wipe the smile from my face. Rip nosed out of the water skin and handed me my sandwich from my apron. I bit into the somewhat smushed bread and inhaled the scent of the food. I adjusted my position to scarf the food down faster, and my notebook fell out of my pocket. It was waterlogged, and all the pages were stuck together in one giant heap. I grimaced and tried to separate the pages. Rip knelt forward and touched the tip of his nose to the front.

Water began pouring from the notebook. The pages dried and flattened until the notebook looked exactly like it had that morning. "Thanks, Rip," I whispered, flipping through the pages. When I came to the last pages, they weren't empty as I had left them. Scrawled across the top in Rowan's messy handwriting was a letter.

It read:

KAM,

IF YOU'RE READING THIS, IT WORKED! YOU WILL DO WELL ON YOUR OWN. DON'T WORRY ABOUT US; A NEW ERA IS COMING. MAY IT BE LONG AND PROSPEROUS.

GO ENJOY YOUR FREEDOM!

I felt a pang of guilt when I read the last line. Rowan had given up everything to help me. I had left him fatherless and probably friendless. Not everyone would be okay with so much change all at once. No peace could last forever, but I hoped, for his sake, he never had to see another rebellion.

I ate my sandwich in the shadowed alley, eyes glued to the opening. There was so much to see. Could anyone ever truly get used to it all? I was watching a woman haggle with a store owner when a thought crossed my mind.

"What do you eat?" I turned and looked at Rip, who was eyeing my sandwich. I took out a slice of smoked fish and handed it to him. He sniffed it and turned away. "Only raw, I guess?"

He nodded.

We sat quietly, watching the people go about their business. No one knew me, and I knew no one. It was a scary thought, but also freeing. Together, Rip and I watched the sky darken into magnificent purples and pinks that were never painted on Eztenburg's skies. As night fell, I began to look for a place to stay. Fog filled the alleyways and blanketed the new city in mystery.

"Ripple?" I whispered. He appeared beside me. "Can you see anything?"

He nodded.

"Well I can't."

I came to a crossroads and paused. Four choices, four different directions I could go. There was one way in front of me, one to my left, one to my right, and the way I had come. As I stood there, arguing with Ripple about the direction we should go, figures began to emerge.

On my left, a boy came into view. His shoulders stooped with sorrow, and he carried a walking stick. Two other people slowly began to arise from the other paths.

We met in the fog.

Acknowledgments

Unlike when I was writing *Cole*, which I wrote rather quickly during the 2020 quarantine, I wrote most of Kam's story between classes during my Junior year of high school. During math classes, he would be sitting at my elbow, whispering dialogue in my ear. At lunch, he would sit in the empty seat beside me and describe Eztenburg in full detail.

After releasing Cole into the world to be read by all my amazing readers, I prayed and prayed that God would use me. I asked Him to spread my message of hope to as many readers as possible and maybe also let this series pay for college. But after the dust settled a little and the sales began to decline, I really began to pray that He would keep spreading my book. Instead, He sent me sheep to tend. Not literally, of course (John 21:15). He sent me people that I may never have ordinarily reached out to. Genuinely honest and nervous writers who didn't know where to go with their manuscripts. I was, and still am, no expert, but in the words of my dear mother, "God doesn't call the qualified. He qualifies the called."

So what can I say except: I hear you, God.

At some point, I had to stop saying, "Use me like this," or "Please do that, so this can happen." Instead, I had to give up control over my measly talents and just pray, "God, your plan is so much better than my own. Use me however You see fit. If it's to reach kids and sell a million copies, I'll praise you. If it's to help the next C.S. Lewis sell a million copies instead, I'll sing hallelujah anyway." Even if God closes a door, I've got to learn to praise Him in the hallway. God, use *Kam* however you wish, *especially* when it's not how I wanted.

Since *Cole* was published, I have received more support than I ever imagined. My former English teacher has a copy in his desk drawer. My pastor has a copy on his bookshelf. Children all across my hometown now treasure Cole as deeply as I do. I have done book signings and school visits that have allowed me to build relationships with people I would never have ordinarily reached.

I need to give a giant thank you to my parents once again. This whole process could never have happened without you. I would still be lost in the cracks of querying and publisher finding if not for you.

To Abby, who heard it first. Your input was more valuable than I can express. Thanks for all the late nights and for listening as I ranted about my own writing shortcomings.

Ms. Dyer, did you know that nearly all of this book was written in your classroom? I promise I was paying attention most of the time, anyway.

Mrs. Naaktgeboren, thank you for your faithful editing and honest feedback.

Lastly, I need to give a shout-out to my own personal fan club. Ainslee, Anni, Lainie, Sadie, Sarah Kate, and Sophie. You don't know how much I needed your hype. It was your motivation that pushed me to keep editing and keep pushing to make this book *better*, especially when all I wanted was to call it quits.

Piper, I hope you find as much comfort between these pages as I do. I hope your thirst for a good book is quenched, even if just for a moment, by this story. Tenley, your vivid imagination pushes me to keep furthering my own world-building and fantasy pieces; never stop being original. Reese, someday when you are old enough to read, I hope you brush the dust off this manuscript and read this adventure and know how much I love you. Also, tell your dad thanks for letting me use his name.

Photo taken by Olivia Merritt

Grace Edgewood is the author of *The Fog Saga,* which currently includes *Cole Magnus* and *Kam Kovah*. When she's not lost in editing, you can usually find her tucked away in the corner with her nose stuck in a piece of children's literature. She was born and raised in the small town of Sparta, where she currently resides with a thousand hardcovers and her new high school diploma. You can visit her at graceedgewood.com, where she has regular writing updates and even a fan-made section with art from readers like you! You can also find official character profiles and a detailed map with all your favorite places from *The Fog Saga*.

Made in the USA
Columbia, SC
23 August 2023